OREGON BILL
THE COLLECTED YARNS
OF A NORTHWEST ICON

2

OREGON BILL

THE COLLECTED YARNS
OF A
NORTHWEST ICON

BY
ROD FIELDER

FLAPJACK PRESS
BROWNSVILLE, OREGON, 1996

THE AUTHOR WOULD LIKE TO THANK THE BROWNSVILLE
TIMES NEWSPAPER WHERE THESE ESSAYS ORIGINALLY APPEARED.

© 1996 by Rod Fielder
First American Printing
ISBN: 1-855266-47-2

Published by Flapjack Press, 36176 Hwy 228, Brownsville, OR 97327

FOR SARA

FOR BUD AND GERALDINE

FOR KITH AND KIN

FOR JAKE

RUFUS, GRANDMA ROSIE, AND CLETUS, 1930

OREGON BILL:
THE COLLECTED YARNS OF A NORTHWEST ICON

GUMPTION

William Robert (far right) helping the Barnwell family
fall timber and clear land at Thief's Neck near Strong
Station, 1898

LEARNING CURVES

While back I told you folks about the learning curve for Oregon Bill. Takes a while for things to get through my noggin. Actually I was born that way. I inherited this condition from my father William Rufus who got it from his father William Robert.

Both men were killed in the woods.

That's the learning curve in Oregon Bill's family—three generations. I'm the first male in three generations not likely to get killed in the woods. As a family you would not call us real swift on the uptake.

William Robert was killed building the old 101 highway clear down in Humboldt County below Eureka in Northern California. Work was hard to get in Shady Cove where he was born so he took his team down to California and signed on to run a fresno, building a road bed for the highway. A fresno is a small-potatoes, horse-powered, earth-moving scoop. A team of horses sort of drags the fresno across the ground leveling it. The teamster grabs the long handle of the fresno. Then, by main strength and awkwardness, he uses that handle to dump the load.

One night William Robert went out on the right-of-way after supper with his youngest son, my Uncle Cletus. Cletus, then about 10, was holding his Dad's hand while in the other hand he carried a lantern.

There had been a lot of blasting that day and some of the limbs had been blown up into the surrounding trees. One of those limbs, a "widow maker," carefully did just that, leaving a young mother and six kids to take care of themselves.

After the State of California settled up with Grandma Rosy, the widow, Aunt Carrie bellowed out, "$3000 whole dollars? Why, Rosy, yer rich!"

Rich they wasn't. The family had a hard scrabble of it. All six kids picked blackberries in the early summer and sold them by the gallon. They all peeled chittum bark too, prying back their fingernails, doing it until they hurt like sin. Chittum bark was gathered, dried, and sold to agents for drug companies who made laxatives, I think, out of the dried bark.

Out on the loamy river bottom land, they sacked carrots. Ever sacked carrots? It's a bother. You attach the sack to a belt around your waist in front and let the bag hang down between your legs. Then you bend over and shuffle along with your legs spread out while you stuff the sack full of carrots; for a nickel a sack or some such. Come lunch, though, the whole family ran to the river to skinny dip, brothers, sisters, the whole passel.

Dad, being the oldest boy, quit school after the eighth grade and got a man's job to help support the family. Doing first one thing and another he finally ended up falling timber for the Pacific Lumber Co. (the P.L.). He got to be a pretty handy faller and made good money. One of his all-time great partners was a Finn by the name of Gunner LaSalle. In the winter when my Dad was stove up[1] with the cold and would huddle around the fire in a goosepen (a hollow tree or stump), why old Gunner would be stripped to the waist high ballin[2]

---

[1] "Stove up" means to be injured or incapacitated. Every Oregon small town in the late 1940's had a bench on main street where old, stove up loggers could chew tobacco, spit, and swap yarns.

[2] "High ballin" means to work fast and hard. It connotes pushing and taking risks, as in; "he's a high ballin son-of-a-bitch!"

to beat hell. But in the summer Gunner would melt while Dad's muscles would loosen up and he'd be high ballin around to beat the band.

One of Dad's ways of saving a little time was fallin trees all morning and sawing them up to length—"buckin," its called—in the afternoon. But falling trees can knock and scrape other standing trees.

On a wet, cold winter afternoon a tree that had been knocked in the morning silently gave way in the watery earth and fell, crushing Dad into the mud and duff on a side hill up Yeager Creek. His partner tried to saw him out but it was of no use. He died before they could get the stretcher up to him to get him down to the railroad tracks and into camp on the speeder.

Two of my uncles, Merlyn and Irving, took me out on Yeager Creek to see that tree. It was big enough to do the job by a darn sight.

That's the learning curve in Oregon Bill's family— three generations. So if you don't get it on the first go round, be patient with your ownself—the lesson is bound to come round again.

GUMPTION

Some old folks have got more gumption than we ever imagined. Oregon Bill got taught this lesson at his Mother's birthday party. The old girl was 85 just last December.

The family decided to get together for dinner and to swap yarns about Nellie, my Mom, to celebrate the day. We each wrote out our favorite anecdote. Then one of the family illustrated and printed up a booklet real fancy with a hard cover, binding, and everything. We called it *Spilling the Beans*.

The title itself is a story. Money was scarce when Roof and Nellie were raising us children during the 30's and 40's. Mom stretched the food budget by cooking lots of beans, especially red pinto beans, sort of soupy and flavored with bacon rind. We ate 'em with lots of catsup and onions over a slice of bread.

And did we grumble? Did we complain? "What, beans? Not again? Yuk!"

Dad would wink at Mother, grin, and call out in a loud voice, "Nellie, pass those Irish strawberries. Love those Irish strawberries."

One Aunt wrote about our Mother, "Do you remember the time we painted the ceiling in your kitchen? You got tired of climbing up and down off the kitchen table so you said, "Rube, I'll jump and you push the table." Well, you did the jumping and I pushed that table all over the kitchen until we painted that whole ceiling."

You should have seen the grandkids' eyes widen

when they heard the story. That bent, frail, little old lady over there, lipstick smeared and wig slightly tipsy? She jumped up and down on a moving table to paint a ceiling? Awesome!

Someone else wrote about the time Nellie set out in the family fliver[1] but came home in a neighbor's car. Through pursed lips she told Roof he could find the car hung up on a telephone pole down in the Hydesville gulch. Never said another word and never drove again until years later after Dad was killed in the woods accident.

As soon as the family heard the story again at the birthday party we all took up the chant, "Tell us Ma; tell us Ma!"

Slowly that 85 year old birthday girl got to her feet. Leaning on her cane she looked sternly at the audience and spoke fiercely the following words, "There are things about my life you'll *never* know!" And she sat down.

So the next time you're impatient up on Main street with a slow, dawdling, hard-of-hearing old lady whose wig is askew and whose lipstick is smeared slightly, just remember: In her day she may have had more spunk in her little finger than you have in your whole body.

---

[1] A "fliver" is another name for a Model T Ford automobile.

Boston Mills Girls

Way back when Oregon Bill was a youngster of 45 or so, he knew a woman named Myra. Now Myra wanted to become a librarian. Trouble is you had to take a tough test and score well, to get into the program at the librarian factory.

One Saturday night we were all partying when Myra returned from the six-hour librarian program admission tests. Naturally, we all gathered around and asked her how it went.

"Piece of cake," she said, "What they called history, I call current events."

It's a great line, isn't it? Especially if you are pushing fifty and looking to roll the dice on your dreams one more time.

Every time Oregon Bill gets together with his Mother he's reminded of Myra's "current events" line. Hey, Nellie is 85. She's been there.

One of Ma's yarns I get a chuckle out of is the one about those high spirited Boston Mills girls. Seems like over Tangent way the Boston Mills ground oats, wheat, corn and other stuff way back when Brownsville was a young whelp. Every farmer took his stuff there to be ground and everybody brought home, or purchased from the General Store, grain processed in sacks stamped "Boston Mills."

A lot of families washed those sacks with lye soap and used the sacking to make homemade underwear. But even lye soap, as strong as it was, couldn't quite remove "Boston Mills" stamped on the cloth.

That's how girls back then around Brownsville got to be known as "Those Boston Mills girls." Bloomers gave them away every time.

The phrase, "Those Boston Mills girls" was just about like saying, "Oh Yeah, your Mother wears army boots." There was sure a whole lot of gnashing of teeth, renting of garments, and pulling of hair when the phrase was used sincerely. Like I say, they was high spirited.

Nellie, my Mother, also remembers oranges as a Christmas gift. Her Mother, Alma Haight, would crochet a bag for each precious orange and hang them on the Christmas tree for the kids. Also on the tree were pine cones as a Christmas gift for the wild creatures. They took ground corn (Boston Mills' finest, of course), mixed it with suet, stuffed the mixture into each pine cone, then hung them on the family Christmas tree.

A beautiful fir tree would be moved inside the house day before Christmas. Grandma and Grandpa Haight would decorate it with strings of popcorn and cranberries. The tree, you see, was a gift from the parents to the children. The very last step was for Grandpa to put the candles on the tree in the parlor.

After a Christmas Eve dinner and party the whole family was allowed into the parlor to see the tree for the first time. Grandpa would light the candles and stand guard. As soon as a single gift plus an orange was distributed to each family member, the candles were put out and taken off.

Immediately afterwards the tree was taken outside and set up in the yard. On Christmas morning everyone could enjoy the many birds that found their way to the gift tree with its corn and suet pine cone decorations.

What a historical moment—sharing the birthday celebration of Jesus with the birds of the valley. How about that as a "current event" in the pageant of your life?

Sure beats those telltale homemade bloomers, that's for sure!

TURKEY AND THE TREE

When I was a kid, family gatherings were a regular thing in our tribe. Whether it was Fourth of July, a Sunday ball game, a summer swim and picnic, or just a Saturday night feed, why you did it with kinfolk and family friends.

Take 1937, for example. That was the year when the mouth of Little River changed where it entered the bay. It flattened out that year into acres and acres of sandy bottom covered with three or four feet of water when the tide was just right. I think it was Uncle Merlyn that discovered crab by the hundreds in those bay waters at the mouth of Little River. On Saturdays that year during crab season we'd grab the garden rake and a gunny sack, and head for the bay. We'd rake up crab by the sack full.

At one of the Uncles' houses a fire would be built and the crab boiled in a big copper wash tub. Someone baked the french bread. Everybody pitched in to buy the beer and the crab feed was on.

The big question in those years before the war was, "Who is going to have the turkey and who is going to have the tree?" What the family wanted decided was where they were going to gather for Thanksgiving and Christmas because the fixins for pies, among other things, had to be tended to. Pies, you see, are sort of the soul food for Bill's kin.

Now personally, I've never met a pie I didn't like. So it's not like I'm a fussy judge or anything. But I've eaten a lot of pie in my day, and I know a thing or two about what makes 'em good. So pull up a chair. Sit a spell. I'll tell you about good pie. Take mincemeat for starters. No, I don't mean that store-bought, raisin junk they serve these days. I mean old time, venison mincemeat pie. The kind Aunt Reta used to make.

Long after I left home I wrote my Aunt Reta and asked her for her mincemeat pie recipe. Her reply began with the sentence, "Go to the springhouse and fetch a small bowl of milk." The rest of the recipe was measured in bowls. It really knocked me out. Just how many cookbooks do you have that measure ingredients by the bowl? And how long has it been since you fetched anything from the springhouse?

Reta's recipe went on to tell about using all the poor cuts of venison—the neck meat and such—preserved for mincemeat pies.

Reta's December, 1940 apple pie was another of her memorable deserts. Reta and Herb lived in a little house about 20 feet by 20 feet square, just a little bitty house like they built in the Great Depression years. Reta still lives there. Right down on Hoover Street. She always thought that was one of God's better jokes—going through the Great Depression only to wind up living all your adult life in a wee house on Herbert Hoover Street.

Well, on that memorable December Saturday in '40 the whole family was crowded into Aunt Reta's house spilling out of the tiny front room into the kitchen. Reta proudly served everybody pie and coffee. That is, everybody was served pie except her nephew, who was me. Then out of the kitchen she came with a big grin and an even bigger whole apple pie, a birthday present for ten year old me.

It was a classic!

Then there were the 1948 huckleberry pies. WW II was over. They were high ballin in the woods. Everybody was making good money and there was plenty of gasoline for the cars. Late August early September of that year, after the first rain to wash off the dust and spider webs, why the whole family would jump in their cars to caravan over to the coast to pick huckleberries.

Reta's legs by then had played out so she couldn't get around good in the gulches. But the huckleberries set so heavy that year Uncle Herb cut off whole branches heavy with fruit and brought them back to camp for Reta to pick.

Then when us kids came back with buckets full of leaves and spiders, she'd arrange a taut woolen blanket and carefully pour our huckleberries down the blanket letting the wool nap catch the twigs and leaves cleaning the berries.

Aunt Reta, you see, was a large figure—both literally and figuratively—in those family gatherings. She reminded you of a Baldwin apple, doncha know, sort of squat and round.

My Aunt Reta is 92 now and in the hospital. One of these days, perhaps soon now, I imagine she'll be asking the Lord, "Who is going to have the turkey and who is going to have the tree?" And if the Lord wants to lay his lip over a good piece of pie, why he'd better listen up.

CLETUS AND BUCKSHOT

Atavista Farm sits pretty as a picture out on highway 228 just East of greater metropolitan Brownsville. It's obviously true the place is at-a-vista. But it's also true it's a throwback, an atavism functioning among us here today but really built for an earlier time.

Cletus and Buckshot Owsley were both built for an earlier time—about the 1700's, I reckon. Both of them should have been pardners of Daniel Boone or the mountain men in the fur trade. But by a hard trick of the universe they were chosen to live their allotted days in the wrong century—the twentieth.

Buckshot and my Uncle Cletus were born to hunt and trap. One day Aunt Annabelle, then an eighth grader, was called up to the front of the class to explain why young Cletus was absent. "Oh, he's mighty sick," lied Annabelle putting on a long face and looking solemn the way teachers like. "Sick is he," said Goldy Jackson. "Then who is that?" she said, pointing out the window. There for all the world to see was brother Cletus high tailing it over the crest of Pioneer Ridge, frying pan banging from the side of a gunny sack filled with varmint traps. Add a bedroll, a little flour, and Cletus wouldn't be back for a week or so.

Trapping was not exactly a standard part of the fourth grade curriculum, which is what Cletus was then— a fourth grader hell bent on turning the clock of history back 250 years. A real throwback. An atavism right here in Brownsville, Oregon.

Cletus and Buckshot lived to go buck hunting. One

time both of them worked on the landing for Holmes-Eureka Logging Company up behind Newburg. In those days hunting season was two months long. Both Buckshot and Cletus regularly quit their jobs year after year about a week before hunting season and took off for the mountains. They'd both be back looking for work two weeks after the season closed, it took that long to dry and smoke the venison jerky they'd eat by the gunny sack full all winter.

Like as not Cletus would go back to hooktendin and Buckshot as a chaser, the jobs they both had left three months earlier. How their families made out I never knew.

Cletus liked to tell the story about how during the Depression he used to hunt deer for the rich dudes up from California. Five dollars a buck was what he charged. One time he was hunting way down in a deep canyon off South Fork mountain, rain falling in sheets. Cletus had lost his hat somehow in the rain, but he managed to shoot a buck deep in that cold, miserable canyon. He had just rolled that buck over, belly to the down hill side so the guts would fall out easy, when a city dude walked up. "He stood there admiring my buck and I stood there admiring his hat. We made the swap and I high tailed it out of there before that dude could ask me to help pack it out."

Of course, Cletus and Buckshot hunted deer the year around, it was just that during legal season they didn't have to pussy foot around so much. Their downfall came one Spring night when at about two o'clock in the morning Buckshot tossed a little gravel up against Cletus' bedroom window. Out he crawled, gun in hand, to do a little outlawin'.

Wouldn't you know, Henry Knudson, the country game warden, got on their tail after they had that little doe in the trunk of the car and were on their way home. Just to discourage old Knudson some, they touched off a round or two in his direction, more for fun than serious. But Knudson was all serious and no play. The county judge ended up taking the car, taking the guns, and throwing both Cletus and Buckshot in the pokey for ninety days. What saddened Cletus most was the loss of his deer rifle, a Savage wouldn't you know, with a peep sight that just flat out never missed.

So next time you slide over to Crawfordsville, when you pass Atavista Farm, take a moment to ponder how hard it must be to be born out of your time. Neither Cletus or Buckshot ever got a real good grip on the twentieth century and how you do it.

TALKS BROWNSVILLIAN

What we're going to do here today is watch the Pioneer Picnic parade and talk Brownsvillian. Lend an ear and I'll tell you how folks in these parts got to greeting one another with the phrase, "Smells like money to me!"

Every strong family, you know, has its own special phrases and peculiar word usage that set them apart and unify even the shirttail kin. Shoot, there's a whole town in California that has its own official language called "Boont," I believe. Boonville is located in a remote valley West of Ukiah in Northern California and "Boont" is spoken there by the old timers. Well, we don't have our own official language here in Brownsville but we do have a number of peculiar words and phrases. "Smells like money to me," is one of 'em.

The phrase was born at our Pioneer Picnic parade back in 1938. Near the end of those Great Depression years, Buckshot Owsley, Welcome Owsley's dad, got aholt of an old, beat-up dump truck. It was a Reo, doncha know. In its day, that Reo had been a fine and fancy vehicle, or, at least as "fine and fancy" as a dump truck can be. Buckshot went to work on cleaning up that truck and painting it. Worked over a year, he did. Painted it a loud fire-engine red. Replaced every fool piece of nickel and chrome on that machine. It was grand.

Buckshot was as proud as a peacock of that rig he was. And it came to pass that he entered it in that year's Pioneer Picnic parade. But, his drinking pals down at the Boomerang Saloon got wind of Buckshot's plans and laughed their fool heads off. Hooted every time Buckshot came in the place. Everybody knew that Buckshot scratched out his drinkin and poker-playing money hauling manure. Even hauled chicken and hog manure, mighty stinkin stuff when it gets ripe on a hot day. Well, the more those Boomerangers laughed and hooted at Buckshot the stronger he bowed his neck.

Sure enough, Buckshot entered the Picnic parade that fine Saturday in June back in 1938. Loaded hisself the biggest, the stinkiest load of manure he could find. On the rear end of his shiny red Reo dump truck he hung the sign, "Smells like money to me!"

That Buckshot tooted his horn and waved to one and all, the whole length of the parade over to the picnic grounds, big grin spread clear across his mug. Even today, you can get a laugh out of an old timer up on Main Street in the tavern on a Saturday night if you choose the right moment and bellow out good and loud, "Smells like money boys; smells like money to me!"

Sui Generii

Met a professor once that loved to lecture one and all about the idea of *sui generii*, or, one-of-a-kind in American higher education. But, it was plain as day the old windbag didn't know *sui generii* from Adam's off ox. Now, me, I was raised among them critters. Time was when Brownsville was full of *sui generii*. They was common as dirt back when Brownsville was a pup. Take Judge Porter Guthrie, a cousin of mine, as a case in point.

It came in real handy to have one of your own up there as county judge when you or one of your shirttail relatives got hauled into court. Didn't help Uncle Cletus a bit, though, when he and his gang of outlaws got caught spot-lighting deer back in '38. Ol' Porter, the judge, threw the whole gang into the county jug for ninety days.

Years later when my kid brother Jumpy and the 20/ 30 club got hauled up before Judge Porter Guthrie, justice took another turn. Here's Jumpy's yarn:

The good membership of the 20/30 club had a habit of whooping it up out at the Boomerang Saloon after their monthly meetings. They'd all get liquored up pretty good and then raise hell returning to main street Brownsville to grab their cars and straggle on home. Got to be a real nuisance. Course you gotta know that the town and the Boomerang didn't get along real well at anytime and the pressure was on Judge Porter Guthrie to close her down. Trouble was the Boomerang Saloon was just outside the city line so all the city fathers could do was gnash their teeth, rent their garments, and carry-on like that.

But on this particular meeting night Sheriff Bart Spinas met that whole mess of bellowing, waving, tooting 20/30 boys as soon as they stepped into the city limits. Hauled the whole gang up before Judge Porter Guthrie on drunk and disorderly charges plus a D.W.I. or two for those driving cars. The D and D charges were pretty routine but Driving While Intoxicated was a pretty serious record to have hanging around your neck. So the boys sobered up pretty fast when Sheriff Spinas marched them right down to the Judge's chambers next to his hardware store that very night.

Judge Porter Guthrie, he went down the line looking over each member one by one, his bifocals halfway down his nose, his gavel tapping ominously in his hand. Then he started to speak addressing his rambling remarks over the heads of the boys off toward the far corner of the room. Started listing the fine get-up-and-go qualities of the Brownsville forefathers. Rambled on about the sad condition of the Pioneer Cemetery and the many stalwart families interred there, fine family names represented in this court room on this very night.

The boys stopped shuffling after awhile, looked at one another sideways under their eyebrows, keeping their eyes averted from the judge, and asked the silent question, "What the hell is going on here?" Then Jumpy thought he got the drift and whispered loudly to the president to ask Judge Porter Guthrie if they could call an emergency meeting of the 20/30 club right there in his chambers. Sure enough the judge consented and no sooner had the emergency meeting been declared open than Jumpy got hisself recognized by the president and immediately proposed that the 20/30 club meet for two hours next Saturday afternoon to trim, clean, and generally beautify Pioneer Cemetery.

Jumpy no sooner got out the two-hour part when Judge Porter Guthrie cleared his throat with a loud, "Harumpf!" Jumpy promptly amended his own motion upping the ante to eight hours work detail on Saturday next.

Judge Guthrie snorted something between a growl and a cough sounding right agitated. Ol' Jumpy shrugged his shoulders and further amended his motion to call for an eight-hour work detail by the full 20/30 club membership both Saturday *and* Sunday.

Bam!

Down came the Judge's gavel. "Boys, I'll take you at your word. Case Dismissed!"

The Judge was careful to drive up to the cemetery real slow that next weekend to check on the work party. When the 20/30 boys finished up, they found a case of cold beer waiting for them on the running board of one of the cars.

Like I say, those *sui generii* were common as dirt back when Brownsville was a pup.

Scouts Honor

"Scouts honor." Those words always remind me of Welcome Owsley. Welcome joined Boy Scouts for three years once and never got a single badge. That was some record, you know, because they'd give you a badge for damn near anything. Why, if you could tie a sheep shank and a bowlin knot, they'd give you a badge right then and there.

Anyways, we were at Scout meetings playin some steal-the-bacon kind of game outdoors one spring night when a rock came sailing out of the dark and broke off two of Welcome's front teeth slicker than a whistle. Broke 'em off about halfway to a stub. Not one of those kids would fess up to the Scout leader on who threw the rock.

Welcome quit Scouting on the spot. It was a matter of Scouts honor. Claimed he got the best of the deal, though, what with his new lop-sided grin. Said a lop-sided grin drove teachers crazy and didn't hurt none with the fast girls.

A lop-sided grin is a heaven sent omen for any youngster aspiring to become the town rake.

And did he drive the teachers crazy. Come to think of it, though, it was kind of a stand-off—school drove Welcome a little crazy too.

Years later Welcome would tell me, "You know, Bill, when we went to first grade, that very first day it was like we was standin next to a high board fence. Everybody reached over that fence and brought back words, numbers, and other wonderful stuff. I reached over that damned fence too, felt all around, and there was nothing there. Bill, there was nothin there. Even tried to shinny up the damned fence, but the teacher told me to sit down."

Welcome was our hero. He was a first class cut-up in school. But he had a real close call when he got to be a sophomore in high school. He fell in love with geometry.

Did every lick of homework and then some. Used to grab our corrected papers after class to check over his own answers. But not once did he hand in a lick of work. Welcome was scared to death he'd end up with a C or B grade and ruin his record. You see, Welcome wanted to do what no kid had ever done before—not get one single passing grade in school, not even in P.E. for cripes sakes.

And the boys' P.E. teacher was something else. Called Welcome and his gang "cigarette puffin punks." One word led to another until one day Coach challenged Welcome's "cigarette puffin punks" to play the varsity in basketball where you need "good wind to play the game."

The damned fool.

Welcome's C.P.P.'s beat the snot out of the varsity. Coach only lasted about four months after that before the school board ran him out of town.

But, a short time later Welcome left school, too. Here's how it happened.

High school principal called old Welcome into his office right out of the blue. Welcome hadn't done nuthin— nuthin at least we were pretty sure the school didn't know about. Said he wanted to help Welcome figure out when he'd graduate.

When they got through listing the requirements, then adding up Welcome's progress, why it was plain as day—Welcome would be about 36 when he graduated from high school, give or take a term or two.

Seeing the look on Welcome's face, that sly old windbag allowed as how if Buckshot, Welcome's Dad, would sign the papers, why he, the principal, would personally talk the school board into lettin Welcome quit to join the army.

And it came to pass.

In the army Welcome realized he was smarter than most of the educated lieutenants he'd come up against. So he taught himself to read. Taught himself to read from pulp westerns while recuperating in the hospital from the cut he'd received on the throat in a street fight in Tokyo. But that's another yarn.

From that day on Welcome read everything he could get his hands on. Even found himself a second hero in all that reading he done. Welcome's first hero, you know, was Zorba, The Greek. But his second hero was Joseph Campbell. Welcome says I ought to read stuff like *Hero with a Thousand Faces*. Or Gould's *Mismeasurement of Man*. Or Hawking's *A Brief History of Time*.

Lord knows, I try. But that stuff puts me to sleep faster than fancy whiskey.

Welcome gets high on books like that.

BACK TO THE FUTURE

A few years ago President Bill got his wife Hillary to try to whomp up a fancy new health program. The government was gonna flat-out guarantee working stiffs a chance to see a sawbones, or, lay up in the hospital at low cost. Reminds me of health care in the logging town I grew up in. Back in the 40's a logger could get sewn up at the hospital in the morning and taken apart that night in a stud poker game in Wildwood across the river—both services provided by Doc Gianotti, the company sawbones. Ol Doc was mighty cheap over to the hospital, but his services were damned expensive at the poker table.

In those days every mill worker and every brush ape in the woods rented a company house for his family. Paid seven dollars a room and the company mowed the lawn as well as painted the house about every seven years or so. That family bought all its food and clothes at the company store. On Saturday night they'd all troop over to the company movie house then, to the Sweete Shopee over to the company hotel afterwards. When the Mrs. reached term, why they'd all troop over to the company hospital where babies were delivered.

Got a few hospital yarns left over from those years. Hospital stories were easy to come by in a town where every good stiff wind meant widow-makers would be falling in the woods. All the town, even the school classes, would be pretty quiet on days like that waiting to see who might be carried out of the woods, injured or dead.

One story my Dad liked to tell didn't involve a widow-maker but it did involve a large chunk of wood hurled through the air when a falling tree bent another and sent it whipping back. Caught my Dad's partner right in the forehead. Scalped him on the spot.

Dad slapped the hank of hair and hide back on his partner's head and then packed him over the fallen logs a quarter mile down the hill to the railroad. Held his partner in his arms on the speeder all the way to camp. Jumped in the waiting ambulance and rode with his partner the twenty miles to the company hospital. Hustled his partner into the hospital where the Doc took over.

Dad said he relaxed a little then and thought since the day was shot he might as well stay around and see how Doc Gianotti earned a dollar.

Next thing Dad knew he woke up on the floor in the doorway with the nurse patting his hand. He'd fainted dead away just when he was about to get a free sawbones lesson. Even in those days a woodsman never knew when he'd have to re-train for another job.

It was at that same company hospital a few years later that Dad gave up smoking. Gave up hand rolled Bull Durham tobacco, which everyone knew was a tobacco mixture consisting of 50% skunk weed and 50% bull. Well, that's how it got its name. And you never knew what "Durham" meant, did you?" Well, now you do.

Roof, my Dad, had smoked hand rolled Bull Durham cigarettes for twenty-five years when one day a large limb fell out of a tree and crushed his lungs while breaking a few ribs. Laid him up in the company hospital where Doc Gianotti said Dad would have to give up his roll-your-owns for two weeks.

Dad never smoked again. Said giving up coffin nails was a piece of cake. Anybody could do it. Said all you had to do was hoist a forty-pound limb about seventy-five feet into the air and let go. If you catch that limb just right on your ribs you won't feel like smoking for quite awhile.

Piece of cake.

I was just a kid back then and I don't know for sure, but I think those medical services were free to the family. I know we didn't worry about medical bills. We worried for sure about getting Dad out of the woods, but we never worried about a doctor or hospital bill. We all had a universal health card. It was stamped on our butts!

Back to the future, Hillary. Back to the future.

Take a Leak

Our family was beating its way across the high desert in Eastern Oregon back then, when the youngest kid had to take a leak. I pulled over, Pete tumbled out, and everyone collapsed into a stupor caused by the desert heat and the fact we were all tuckered out after a week of hard camping up in the Wallowas. After what seemed like an unusually long time we yelled at Pete to get back in the car. After we were underway someone growled, "why'd you take so long?" Pete replied proudly, "I was practicing writing my name."

Pete, you see, was just days away from starting school and was anxious to get off to a good start. What better way to sneak in a little practice on the high challenge of kindergarten? Good writing instrument. Something you could get your whole being involved in.

One of my all-time goofs when I was young involved taking a leak. I was away at college at the time and the fall of my freshman year I was invited to a sorority ball. This was capital P Posh out at the country club—a full orchestra, orchids all around, the works. All the sorority girls were elegantly coiffed and decked out in several hundred dollars worth of fancy gowns. Every guy had rented a tuxedo and even had put on the cumberbund. I mean it was straight out of *The Great Gatsby*, "...the rich are different than you and I," that sort of scene.

Well, you can imagine the all-eyes silence that swept the tables around the dance floor when my date, also a freshman, excused herself, made a wrong turn and swept grandly into the men's room. And she stayed there. Panicked, I guess. The world stopped for about seven eons of time until she emerged.

I acted like just about everyone else—embarrassed, big time. Even avoided her on campus til the end of the term. She never came back to school after Christmas break.

It was like my Aunty Ruby said, "Bill, you acted like the South end of a horse going North!" True enough. And because Aunt Ruby was normally such a generous, joyful soul your neck snapped to and your head came 'round when she saw fit to compare her nephew favorably with a horse's patoot! But I was only seventeen at the time. What can ya expect?

Now, my Great Grandfather, William Ridge, he was eighty years old when he took his famous leak. Here's the yarn. Seems like it was Ridge's and Tennessee's fiftieth wedding anniversary. Somehow, Tennessee had gotten Ridge and herself off the ranch on one pretext or another. But she had arranged for everyone to be out at the old home place just ahead of them when they were to arrive back. Everybody brought in the cake and punch, hid the Model T's, and crouched on the front porch when, sure enough, they saw the lights of the Dodge touring car flash up the lane. Tennessee got out and sauntered up to the porch. Great Grandpa Ridge, as he always did, stopped to take a leak by his customary tree. He was just in full stream when the lights went on and forty-five of their kids and kin all jumped out and shouted, "Happy Anniversary!"

Old Ridge was cool. He finished up, shook it out, put the horse in the barn and turned to greet his guests with a big grin stretched clear across his mug.

In the family these shenanigans are believed to be caused by the "horses patoot gene." It's recessive, you know, and only comes out in males in the family every second generation or so. But those gene carriers are something else. Take the time Bill his ownself was standing on a stump and had to take a leak. But that's another yarn.

BEING A KID

Oregon Bill, sister Chub, and brother Lee or Jumpy
(left to right) diving into the Calapooia River, 1940

Baby Bottoms

I wasn't actually raised in a company town like my cousins were. But my Dad was a chopper[1] for the outfit that owned the company town right down to the hospital. Pat Doyle claimed that the company doctor branded the butt of every kid born in that hospital with the initials "P.L." so there wouldn't be any confusion about the assets of the Pacific Lumber Company.

Folks rented their houses from the company for seven dollars a room. P.L. took care of everything; electricity, water, the works, even mowing lawns all summer and painting the house about every seven years. At one time the P.L. issued their own script money which you could spend at the company store, at the Sweete Shoppe, in the company hotel, or down at the company movie theater over by Mill B.

That movie theater had great pillars out front made of whole logs set upright with the bark still on. It looked a little like Greek columns. At Christmas time those columns were garlanded with tree boughs and wreaths. On the Saturday before Christmas, we kids shivered with excitement waiting in the cold fog and rain for a special holiday show. We all filed in, took our seats, and gawked at the huge tree down front. There it was, a floor-to-ceiling Douglas Fir which the bosses and their wives had decorated the night before.

---

[1] A "chopper" is a lumberjack, a timber faller. Choppers are also called "cutters" and even "brush apes" but only by fellow loggers.

After the cartoons, probably Looney Tunes, the curtains were drawn back and there on the stage were thousands of toys stacked high on shelves. Not plastic junk. These were five-dollar toys back in the times when you could pull into the Piggly Wiggly and feed a family of six for a week on that kind of money.

Mothers with babes in arms went first while the big kids like us wriggled in our seats, whispered furiously, and pointed to the several presents we'd have to choose from—the Tom Mix pistols with buckskin fringed holsters or a set of Lincoln Logs? I mean these were tough choices. So the mothers walked down the aisles and up across the stage where they pointed to a teddy bear or some such and one of the bosses, perhaps Derby Bingdorf himself, would take it off the shelf and present it to her.

These occasions were always a little unsettling since bosses during the 30's were like royalty and you tried to have as little truck with them as possible since 200 men or so waited outside the mill every day hoping someone would get canned.

Off the stage you'd walk with your five-dollar gift, probably your BIG GIFT that Christmas, personally handed to you by a boss. At the side door as you exited from the stage, a big bag of hard candy was given to each kid.

They tried to organize the P.L. several times and there were bitter strikes in the 30's and 40's. It's really hard to go out on strike, though, when the key to your house is owned by the company and the bosses all play Santa Claus at Christmas time.

Teaching Brother Lee to Fly

For some reason Ma named her youngest son Carol Lee. That name lasted just long enough for Carol Lee to get himself big enough to insist his name was Lee. Period. But before Carol Lee became Lee we almost taught him to fly.

Brother Lee had red hair and a fair complexion. It was the fair complexion, I think, that made it murder when he got a good dose of poison oak. That boy broke out in a rash if he got anywhere near poison oak. But, being a kid playing outdoors he was forever rubbing up against the stuff. Great huge red welts would bust out all over his body. Ma would strip him naked and stand him up on the kitchen table where he would howl and dance while Ma daubed Kalomine Lotion (or sometimes vinegar, I think) on those swollen red welts all over his body. The rest of us kids stood there with our mouths hanging open watching Lee's naked howling dance. Only later did we figure out how Lee could fly like Superman.

Lee was the youngest kid in our family and listening to the radio at four o'clock every afternoon convinced him he could fly like Superman. One day he put on a red and blue cape my sister Chub used marching around the W.O.W. Hall uptown Saturday mornings at the *Junior Woodmen of the World* club meetings. Lee put on Chub's cape and took off running flat-out through the dining room and on into the parlor. He hit the sofa on a dead run and bounced off that couch right through the window shattering glass all over the front porch. Carol Lee barely got a scratch. Man of steel!

This boy was serious about flying.

Out Seven Mile Lane our house had a very high back porch. From this porch Mother used to hang her washing on a long line with a pulley on either end. She'd hang out a pair of bib overalls pinning it to the line with clothes pins. Then she'd pull the line out a few feet and pin up another pair of overalls. This was repeated until all the clothes were hung on the pulley line.

The Krypton Kid, my brother Carol Lee, wanted badly to fly just like Superman. So we got this idea. We would pin him to the clothes line just like a pair of bib overalls. We would all pull like mad on the line, and Carol Lee would go flying across the yard, cape fluttering just like Superman.

Great idea, huh? Carol Lee was so small and so skinny he'd fly with no effort at all.

Cinchy. You can do it.

We talked Carol Lee into climbing up on the porch rail. We pinned him to the line. Even used extra clothes pins. When the Krypton Kid was ready, we all gave a big yank on the clothes line jerking Carol Lee off the porch rail. He fell ten or twelve feet breaking his arm.

We all ran like hell to find Ma and tell on Carol Lee.

BEING A KID

Actually, what we're talking about here is being a kid in the 30's right here in Brownsville. It starts with a life and death struggle.

The struggle to survive started just as soon as you got out of bed. Hopping up and down on one foot and then another in the wet cold Oregon winter morning you fought the daily mystery—how to untangle the long johns. Long johns you know have a back flap in the seat and one leg or arm of the long johns always got wrong side out and stuck through the back flap. Doesn't sound like much, but for a half-asleep ten-year-old on a cold morning it was a formidable intellectual challenge. That's why all the sixty-year-olds are so smart here in Brownsville today. The dumb ones never made it past their tenth birthday back during the hard scrabble '30s. Many a nine-year-old was found blue on the floor with only one pitiful little arm or leg sticking in the long johns.

Every morning mothers drug survivors out from under the bed, out of the closet, or wherever they were hiding and stuck a teaspoon of cod liver oil down their gullet. No matter how you wiggled, no matter how you gagged, no matter how you dry heaved, down it went. Come hell or high water you had to choke that miserable stuff down. What was worse you belched cod liver all morning and wretched that oil back up to taste it again.

We got a dab of orange with our cod liver oil. To this day I gag a little at the remembered cod liver oil taste associated with oranges.

Then it was off to school.

Because we were Depression kids we lined up by classes down at the cafeteria to march by a box of fruit the government was buying from farmers to boost prices. One week we got two handfuls of dried Oregon prunes from down in Douglass County or up near Dallas. The next week we got grapefruit from California. Learned to peel and eat grapefruit like oranges only they didn't have the cod liver oil taste.

During recess we played bottle tops. You remember how a bottle was delivered to your back door every morning by the milkman. And that bottle was sealed with a round disk of cardboard. We saved those cardboard disks and Welcome Owsley and I would challenge big kids to slap their bottle top down on the sidewalk. The winner was the guy who could slap his bottle top down on the other guy's top. Winner took all the bottle tops that had been slapped down.

Welcome and I were probably the best bottle top slappers ever. Even beat those suckers in the eighth grade and then ran like hell cause nobody likes to be beat by fifth grade twerps.

After school we raced our orange crate racers on the cement sidewalks down Spaulding Street. We made our orange crate racers by stealing one of our sister's roller skates. Took a wrench and loosened the adjustable slide and took the front wheels and back wheels apart. Then we nailed those wheels on a 2 x 4 stud about three feet long. On one end of the 2 x 4 you nailed an upright orange crate. Then you nailed on handles and you had a kind of home-made scooter you could whiz down the street racing Joe Hogan, Festus

House, or Welcome Owsley to the end of the block.

And popcicles. Do you know about Depression popcicles? Well, over at the General Store they had a new fangled refrigerator. Probably the only one in town. Use to put kool aid into the ice trays. When the trays were about half frozen, old man Cooper would stick little tooth picks into each kool aid cube. Yep, for two cents you could buy yourself a grape popcicle. Best flavor goin.

Every kid back then wore bib overalls and high top shoes. Belted pants and low cut shoes meant you were no longer a kid. You were ready for work.

And we thought we was rich. Always wondered how poor kids were gettin along.

BIG AND LOTS

Logger sons don't have no truck with little or less. No sir, in all the important things in life—fallin timber, huntin bucks, playing Sunday ball, and makin love—only two things really count: BIG and LOTS. Well, I take that back—FAST counts when you're up against a good pitcher (but not when you go for a roll in the hay).

Got two yarns just in case any slow learners out there never got the word about BIG and LOTS in the lives of men folk.

After my grandfather was killed in the woods, Rufus, his son (my father,) was sent down to Mendocino on the Northern coast of California to work in the woods. Young Roof was still wet behind the ears but he was tall for his age, had big hands and a barrel chest. Why he was sent to Mendocino I never knew. Probably some shirt-tail cousin already worked there. You know, "write if you get work," that sort of deal.

Anyway, Roof was lollygaggin by the cookhouse that first day after work in the woods when someone came up behind him, pulled his hat down over his eyes, spun him around, and clipped him neatly on the chin knocking him ass over tea kettle.

A minute later those same hands helped him up and walked him over to the horse trough where he was told to clean himself up.

"No hard feelins, son," said the helper, "but I'm the Bull here because I can whip any man in camp. You were just big enough to raise a little doubt 'mongst these brush apes. Now, lets you and me go get us some of Cookie's vittles."

"Just big enough to raise a little doubt." A pretty good teacher, huh? But teaching about BIG really begins with homework. Homework like your Aunties saying, "My what a BIG boy," or your Uncles asking you to show how BIG the biceps are in your arm. Yes sir, the BIG lesson starts early and doesn't let up. It even slops over into pie helpings.

Now, personally, I just never have met a pie I didn't like. This passion of mine started early and I got a reputation in the family. The day I turned 10 we went over on Hoover Street to visit Uncle Herb and Aunt Reta. "Hoover Street," everyone got a big laugh out of that one—imagine calling Hoover Street home during the Depression! Uncle Herb used to do a little cowboying when he was young but now he pulled green chain down at the mill for Holmes Eureka. Reta, his wife, cooked the best pies in the whole county. Well, that Sunday—you always visited kin on Sundays—when Aunt Reta brought around the coffee and pie, she left me out! Then, out of the kitchen she came, lips stretched clear 'cross her face in a big grin, and plopped down in front of me a whole apple pie; I mean, we're talkin a whole apple pie of my very own, age 10. Yes sir, I knew BIG and I knew I was gettin there. Aunt Reta could not have made it more plain.

The BIG lessons were still goin after I reached 17 or so. Here's the yarn.

Summers I started workin on the engineering crew for the P.L. Lumber Company. We ran property lines, chopping lines, too, to lay out where the fallers would cut the timber. We did railroad beds and truck roads —all the necessary planning that needs to be carried out about three years ahead of the logging.

The engineering crew was a dream job for a kid. Walking in the woods every day and eating lunch in an old growth forest. Even carried a little hand axe for cutting brush to clear a line-of-sight for the chief-of-party looking through the transit measuring angles. Sometimes, just for fun, I'd take my axe and shave down a sort of shingle. Then I'd write on that shingle, "Save For Roof". I'd tack that shingle sign up on the biggest and tallest tree (get that BIG idea there?) I could find, hoping Dad would find it on his layout (a "layout" or "show" is the strip of land a pair of fallers are assigned to fall timber), or, even better, a rival faller would find the sign and get hot under the collar seeing that the biggest and best timber had already been claimed.

Came back to one of my signs a day later to find that a bear had taken a swipe and knocked that Rufus shingle clean off the tree. No doubt at all about who Mr. Bear thought was BIG in that neck of the woods.

One time engineering, I was standing there on a big stump holding a back sight for the transit man and I had to take a whiz. I put down my plumb bob, walked over to the edge of the stump, and was standing there passing my water. Down the mountain rolled the bellow of a faller up the hill from me. "Would you look at that young buck. He's got to stand on a stump to keep it out of the mud!"

So much for BIG. Stick around and I'll teach you about LOTS.

Shovels, Inc.

This is a yarn about the titanic corporate wars between the Great Earth Moving Company and Shovels Incorporated. Both companies existed only in Oregon Bill's eleven-year-old mind. This and other imaginings will be revealed shortly.

But first I have to give you the whole skinny about small-town Oregon life in the '40s.

Most kids my age (eleven) in small Oregon logging towns began taking responsibility for a new going-to-church-on-Easter outfit—slacks and sport coat, in my case—during the '40s. You were looking at 20, maybe 25, whole dollars for new duds. Not a humongous amount of money but a fair poke, especially considering you got only one dollar for working eight hours at the hardware store on Saturday. You made up for Saturday's low pay, though, when you got a whole fifty-cent piece for just two hours work after school. Yep, $2.50 was my weekly wage for eighteen hours work at Judge Grunewald's hardware store. Course there was no social security or income tax taken out.

But there were other advantages.

Like education.

Old Judge Grunewald, the owner and part-time county judge, would fondle and pinch the twenty-year-old sales girls when he'd pass them in the narrow aisles back between the horse collars and the varmit traps. Judge G's wife would fire those girls just as fast as he could hire them. But not before the girls would confide in me about the carryings-on of the licentious old coot.

Back then spring gardening worked hand-in-glove with the season of new Easter duds. You see, in those days everybody in town grew a big vegetable garden. And in the weeks before Easter every widow lady on a pension, every stove-up logger, every school marm, and everybody too prissy or proud to get their hands dirty all needed their garden spaded. They hired us kids for fifty cents an hour to turn the sod.

It was boring work and hard on the back if the ground was wet or a heavy clay. So to make the hours roll by I'd take my shovel point and mark out a rectangle on the surface of the unspaded soil.

Here's where those two entrepreneurial giants, Great Earth Moving and Shovels Inc., would come into play. Both firms would bid aggressively on how many shovel fulls it would take to spade that rectangle, low bidder or fewest shovel fulls winning the contract. Under bidding meant your shovel man (me) had to lift some mighty big shovel fulls.

Damn near got a hernia making good on some of those contracts! But the hours roll by when you make believe you are guiding the fiscal destiny of G.E.M. Co. in its never ending industrial wars with its arch rival, Shovels, Inc.

Another way for a kid to make money for Easter clothes was to go up town and set pins at the bowling alley—ten cents a line. In those days there were no automatic pin setters. No sir. Ten-year-old boys would perch on a little shelf down there above all the pins, set them in the frame, hit a button, and the frame would move down and back, setting up all the pins. You'd jump up on the ledge out of the way of some drunk logger who would laugh like hell if he could catch you with his bowling ball if you were still in the pit when his ball hit the pins.

Actually, it was no place for a kid.

The bowling alley was separated from the bar by a swinging door. It could get dicey when the bar patrons decided to bowl a line or two. It was especially dangerous when my Cousin Melvin got liquored up and wanted to throw his special order, two hundred pound bowling ball—well, it seemed that heavy to me—through the brick wall at the back of the padded pit. Pins would blast every which way, some of them clear into the next alley over. Cousin Melvin was all muscle and booze.

I'd hustle those pins like mad, thinking all the while of the things I'd do to Cousin Melvin when I outgrew him and outmuscled him. I knew for darn sure that even at age 10 I could outthink Melvin even when he was sober.

But, in fact, I never grew that much or muscled up. And I've never bowled a line. Not one. Anyway, Cousin Melvin died young. Undiagnosed, premature altzheimers, I think got him.

BEING HANDY

Folks just don't use the word "handy" like they used to. Used to be that statements like, "He's handy with an axe," or, "She's handy with milk cows" was honest praise. "Expertise" is the fluffy word we use today. Sorta makes me gag.

Now my old man Roof, short for Rufus, was pretty handy with an axe. His hands were big and they hung out of his sleeves like sledgehammers with thumbs. And they were black, those hands; stained that way by the sap in the redwood trees he fell and bucked. But what knocked me out about the sight of those hands were the cuts. His hands were forever getting scraped, nicked, gouged, and occasionally cut real deep. Roof would often put pitch on the cut to staunch the flow of blood, then go on working—with his hands.

Then there was the stubbed-off finger Roof lost back to the first joint when he caught it in a washer wringer when he was a kid. That stubbed-off finger was the cause of my downfall. I just didn't see how he could beat me when I challenged him to play marbles for keeps. Shoot, if the stubbed finger wasn't enough then the danged marbles would probably stick to the pitch on those gnarly big hands.

See, I was pretty handy myself. Handy at playing marbles for keeps. When you play marbles for keeps it's best to play with the older kids. Oh, they might try to catch you and whomp you after school, but they're not likely to bawl and tell the teacher to get you in trouble. Welcome Owsley and I regularly counted up winnings of 20 to 30 marbles a day. We even beat a lot of the big eighth graders.

Naturally I had to challenge my old man one night after work. We lagged and sure enough I won and got to shoot first. I hunkered down on the rim of the circle drawn on the smooth ground with my number one, all-time favorite shooter, a green "clearie" in hand. Knocked one out of the circle on my first shot. But I didn't "stick." You see, if you shoot real hard and you hit another marble dead center, you'll stick right in that spot probably close to other marbles to knock out of the circle. So I had to shoot from the rim again. I missed that second shot and that was it. She was all over.

Roof got his big black, pitch encrusted fist down on the circle and whacked out a marble with his first shot, stubbed off finger and all. I didn't think he could even fold that sledgehammer fist around something as small as a marble. There was no way he could shoot with the stubbed finger. No way.

Lucky him. His first shot stuck. So did his second. He was shooting from inside the circle, often no more than 6 to 10 inches away from the target marble he chose to knock out of the circle. My shots from the circumference had been 15 to 20 inches away.

Cleaned me out.

Must have been pretty handy with a marble when he was a kid.

Rubber Gun Wars

Come the first warm Saturday in Spring our gang always showed up at Doc Comfort's place. Isn't that a kick? A doctor named Comfort. Just sounds like everything is going to be alright no matter how big that tree was that fell on you.

Doc had two boys and they took the lead in the great rubber gun wars back on that warm Saturday in the Spring of 1940. See, back then every tire had an inner tube made of real rubber you could cut up into half-inch-wide rubber bands. It was rubber that would stretch over sticks, and when you pulled them back real far then let go they would zip thirty feet or so. It was a bigger version of the little rubber gun wars you had in school with small bands stretched over your pointing finger.

For our rubber gun wars we each whittled a long rifle with a jack knife. We put a shallow notch at the very end of the barrel to hold the rubber band; then we cut a notch back near our nose on the top of the gun barrel. You'd stretch an inner tube rubber band back along the barrel and catch it in the notch. When you ran around the house and caught one of the Comfort boys you'd nudge that rubber band out of its notch. Off it would zip to catch Jerry or Phil, or somebody, upside the head.

"You're dead!"

"No, I'm not!"

"Yes, you are."

And so on.

We made rubber gun pistols and rubber gun machine guns. For the pistol you'd strap a clothes pin vertically on the rear of your gun. Then you'd stretch a rubber band back along the barrel and slip it into the jaws of the clothes pin to hold it. Pressing the clothes pin would open the jaws releasing the rubber band to zip into someone's face. Machine guns were made by laying a string over five or ten notches. Rubber bands were stretched to catch in each notch. By pulling up the string, you'd pull each band out of its notch and they'd all go zipping off rat-tat-tat.

Rubber gun wars up at Doc Comfort's place were great that Spring of 1940.

The weapon we never told our folks about was our grooved arrow shooters, a variation on the rubber gun. In this case you'd use the grooved side of a tongue-and-groove board to whittle a wooden rifle. Into the groove you slipped a 10-inch-long pointed arrow made from a piece of shingle. The thick part of the shingle was the pointed front of the arrow; while on the thin part of the shingle-arrow you'd whittle a kind of upright airplane tail. Back along the groove holding the shingle-arrow you'd stretch a thick inner tube rubber band. When you'd release the rubber band it caught the shingle-arrow and sent it whizzing down the groove. Our arrow shooters were pretty lethal and reasonably accurate up to fifty or seventy-five feet. Used 'em to shoot holes in our homemade kites.

Kite wars were another spring passion for 10-year old boys around Brownsville in those days. Used to sharpen the end points of our three-sticker homemade kites then try to maneuver 'em so as to catch and rip somebody else's kite. Or, we'd grind up glass and glue it to a section of string then "saw" the other guy's string and cut his kite loose to sail over the top of Welcome Owsley's house.

But every Sunday we'd show up to usher in folks at the Methodist Church. We'd look pious as hell, even coming back to church Sunday evening for M.Y.F. (Methodist Youth Fellowship). The natural attraction there was playing kissing games with the girls over at Bubby Jackson's barn after the meeting until we had to run like mad to get home before the nine-thirty curfew.

All in all we were probably better at the rubber gun wars than the kissing games. Except for Welcome Owsley. But that's another yarn.

Who Can You Trust?

Late in the Depression years my dad got laid off by the P.L. Company. So he hooked on, with Holmes Eureka Co. logging out on the VanDuzen River. We camped that whole summer at Grizzley Creek in a grove of old growth redwoods whose great root systems humped up out of the ground two feet or more near the base of the tree. Dad took his axe and cut out little bench seats for all six of the family in the semi-circle made by the base of the tree and two of those huge root systems. Out in front of these seats he built a little rock fireplace for the evening bonfire.

That was the summer of 1938, the summer Campfire Marshmallows came out with coconut coating. We had a bonfire every night and roasted marshmallows probably once a week while the VanDuzen River breeze soughed high in the sweeping branches of that ancient grove.

My Uncle Merlyn made me a yew wood bow that summer I was eight. Not an English long-bow, but an Osage Indian bow, short and flat. He backed it with rawhide to aid the wood in its spring back to straighten itself and fling the arrow. It was a wonder.

But as wondrous as that bow was, I could never shoot an arrow to fly higher than the crowns of those old growth trees. They were that high and more. High enough, you know, to sweep droplets out of the fog and make rain where there was none.

We swam in the VanDuzen most evenings after Dad got off work and all day on the weekends. Dad would toss white pebbles into the clear water and all four kids would pile into the river, diving to the bottom to see who could retrieve them first.

We loved it. Purely.

In camp one hot August day us kids decided we just couldn't wait for Dad to get back from the woods. We just had to go swimming.

"Please Mom," we begged. "All we want to do is just go look!" It took an hour or two, but we finally wore her down and she let us go to the river, "just to look."

As soon as we got out of camp we got our heads together to hatch a plan. We just knew Ma couldn't catch and spank all four of us. No way. So we came up with this plan, see, and everybody agreed. One for all; all for one.

The plan was to stand on the bank all holding hands. We would count to three then all jump in.

Simplicity itself.

Absolutely fool proof.

Only, it didn't work.

Yvonne, the oldest led the count with Chub, my sister, and Lee, my little brother, chiming in grinning from ear to ear. I was on the opposite end of the line from Yvonne.

One!

Two!

Threeee!

And I ended up way out in the middle of that river. All by myself.

Spent a week in the boy's tent. Didn't even get to come out to eat; only to pee.

If you can't trust your own kin, who can you trust?

STEAMY SEX

I mean steamy sex is used to sell everything from underwear to mouthwash. So, hold right there. We're gonna get physical. Oregon Bill is gonna lay out the straight skinny about bird and bee stuff. We'll sell us a bunch of whatever.

First, I have to get technical. Ever heard of a goosepen? You know, like the phrase, "We'll hole up in that goosepen over there 'til the weather eases up." You see, when a fire sweeps through an old growth forest, often it doesn't do a lot of real damage except that here and there the fire can get in at the roots of a tree and slowly burn out any rot in the core. In a very large, very old tree like one of the redwoods down on the southern Oregon coast it can burn out a small room with its own crawl-through door. That's called a goosepen.

Most logger aunties and grandmothers will tell you a goosepen is where logger sons are properly found. They are found there along with similar young varmits like bear cubs, wildcats, and such. Normal folk are born in homes or hospitals, but not logger sons.

Where logger daughters come from I never learned.

Aunt Delia and my father shared a birthday so we used to go to her house of a Sunday. Aunt Delia would fix chicken and dumplings for her favorite nephew, Roof. After dinner we'd all sit in the parlor and listen to the old folks swap yarns about falling timber, playing baseball, and hunting deer.

Out of the blue on Sunday Aunt Delia turned to me and asked, "Bill, do you ever pee in the bathtub?" What a dumb question. And shocking too. "When you are soaking in the tub and you have to pee, what do you do, Bill? You don't jump out of the tub getting the floor all wet do you?" the old girl went on.

I mean, how do you deal with mischievous aunts like that when you are only ten years old? And it's Sunday in the parlor for cripes sake.

But the Methodist Church had the liveliest sex education course around. On Sunday nights we had M.Y.F., Methodist Youth Fellowship for teenagers. Never missed a Sunday. No, sir, because we'd play "Wink-um." Chairs would be put in a circle and all the girls would be seated with a boy standing behind each girl. Except that one boy would have an empty chair. That kid would look here and there and offer a quick, sly, or rapid wink around the circle. If the girl could get her bottom off the chair before the guy behind her could tap her shoulder, then that girl could waltz over to her new guy's empty chair.

It was hot stuff on Sunday night.

After M.Y.F. we all went over to Bubby Jackson's place and played kissing games that warm spring of '41. Then Welcome Owsley and I would walk the Andrews sisters to their house up Blakely Street singing, of course, "Walkin My Baby Back Home." Gee, but it was great.

Like every generation, we thought our gang had invented just about all there was to know about steamy sex. But it was my sister, Chub, who asked the brilliant question of an earlier generation. Chub asked Aunt Dorothy, "Did you ever do anything naughty when you were young?"

"Naturally," replied Aunt Dorothy. "We were flappers, you know. Like one summer night we had a bonfire on the Calapooia River. It was way up by the Swiss

Cheese swimming hole. We were going to have a weenie roast. You remember how weenies used to be linked together in long strings? I told everybody I'd show them how to roast seenies. I took off all my clothes. Wrapped those weenies around my body. Then I danced around the bonfire roasting weenies."

I was 60 years old before my sister told me that nifty story about Aunt Dorothy. "Naturally. We were flappers, you know." What a great line.

Roasting weenies on the Calapooia. Grin just stretches clear across your mug for the imagining, doesn't it?

GOOBER PEA

William Rufus, (lower left), and the Brownsville baseball team, 1916

SORE ARM CATCHERS

All right flatlanders, we're goin to play a little Sunday ball. All jump in the fliver and we'll drive over to Crawfordsville. Park the rig down the third base line. Sit on the front fender and honk the horn good when Oregon Bill gets a hit. After the ball game we'll picnic down on the Calapooia River and then go for a swim.

Bubby Jackson, my old time manager, always claimed we'd have a great ball club if only we could just find a few more red-wine-drinkin, goin-to-confession, Eyetalians. Bubby said no one could throw harder, run faster, or hit the long ball like those guys. Didn't want no more slow-footed, sore-armed, short-ball hittin Methodists like me.

Don't know what he was complaining about. Cacci already played third. Capanna in right, Cezaretti in left, and Senestrero in center. Gionotti played short and Francesconi was on the mound. All we had to do was change Red Oliver's name to "Oliveroni" and me to "Billarducci" and we'd be formidable—an all Eyetalian line-up.

What really stuck in Bubby's craw was my sore arm. I think I was born with it. Rufus, my pop, couldn't understand how he had sired a sore arm catcher. In his day he could throw the blamed ball through a brick wall. Secretly, I think he thought there had been a switch in babies down at the company hospital. Only, right there on my ass was the brand the company doc put on all babies—P.L.—for the Pacific Lumber Company.

So the constant sore arm was one of God's mysteries for my father.

One winter Rufus came up with the idea of not touching a baseball. "Don't throw for six months; rest that arm totally. Come summer you'll have a rifle up your sleeve." Summer came. No rifle.

Next winter he said, "We'll throw every day. Don't let those adhesions form on the tendons. When summer comes around you'll have a cannon up your sleeve." Summer came. No cannon.

The next winter was the winter of the ten-pound all-wool sweatshirt. Wool retains warmth even when wet, you know. "Keeps those muscles loose," said Roof. "Next summer you'll have a bazooka up your sleeve." Summer came. No bazooka.

As a sore arm catcher, Oregon Bill had two all-time low points. The first came while playing college ball in the Bay Area one spring and coming up against a tough pitcher in Stanford's sunken diamond. I hit two doubles and a home run, but Stanford stole some ungodly number of bases off me—think it was fourteen when the dust cleared. As old Bubby said afterwards, "Bill, they stole everything but your jock."

Another low point was playing Fresno State. It was a hot bed of baseball then, and we played home games out at Civic Stadium where the back stop and box seats set in real close to home plate. A big, old time, leather-lung rabid fan sat right behind home plate. Second inning he started in on me.

"Here comes old rubber arm. Hey folks, watch the rainbow to second."

"Way to go, rubber arm."

Fresno State went wild on the bases. Fibber Hirayama

stole four of them by himself. I got two of our team's
three hits, but I still felt like joining the Catholic church
and looking for a dad named Dimaggio.

Maybe they could perform a gene splice.

Now catching for Brownsville—Bill Dimaggio, Jr.

Play Ball

Have you ever shaken hands with an old-time base-ball catcher?   Those burly fingers broken by tipped fast balls slant every which way. It's something like grabbing a brush pile. You know you've got a hold of something, but it's hard to get a real grip.

My dad was an old-time catcher who played Sunday ball for years on teams sponsored by local logging outfits. During the week he was a faller working in the woods. On Sundays he swung a bat instead of a double-bitted axe.

To give the old man his due, I guess he was a pretty fair hitter. During the 40's, long after he'd stopped playing, the old gaffer organized and managed a baseball team so me and another kid, the son of a baseball buddy, could play ball when teams and leagues were in short supply. On Sunday Dad put himself into the line-up when we were short a player. He hit four automatic doubles that day about 325 feet into the apple orchard in short right field. I struck out three times.

Men then talked of only three things, or so it seemed —playing ball, buck hunting, and falling timber. Oh, they might give Herbert Hoover hell long into the 40's, but politics was not a subject they dedicated their lives to like they did with timber, horns, and horsehide.

One of the well-told stories was how Roof, short for Rufus, my dad, knocked the umpire out with a low throw to second. Before Roof hurt his arm, he had a rifle up his sleeve. He threw to second so hard that the ball went low over the pitcher's mound and started to rise as it reached second base. Well, one Sunday only one umpire showed up so he had to call balls and strikes from behind the pitcher's mound. Sure enough a man stole second. The umpire turned and crouched to make the call. Roof's throw caught him right behind the ear. Coldcocked him on the spot.

Like I told you. I was a kid listening to these stories and I thought to myself, "Yeah Dad; sure you did; baloney!"

As it turned out I played ball in college. One Saturday I caught the second game of a double header and an old time umpire asked me in the first inning, "Waddya say yer name was kid?" I told him. Third inning he says, "Any of your family play ball in Linn County, Oregon?" And he named my home town 200 miles away. In the seventh inning he said, "Tell you about the time I got knocked out by a hard throwing catcher over to Sodyville up there in Oregon." And he told me about a young logger who used to play ball on Sunday with a rifle up his sleeve.

And I thought to myself, "Yeah, Roof, you sure did."

GOOBER PEA

Let me tell you a family story about the goober pea. The story starts about 1932, building the dam at Prospect, Oregon. No work in the woods so Roof, my dad, got a W.P.A. job pushing an Irish baby buggy—a wheel barrow—to lug cement in and build that dam.

On Sundays Roof caught Big George, a fast ball pitcher for Medford in the old Southern Oregon League. Big George could pitch well enough to take Medford to the championship game, which they lost to Grants Pass that year. He was a Texan and called the peanut a goober pea. That tickled my dad. He flat out giggled every time Big George called for goober peas in that Texas twang of his when laughs were hard to come by during those hard-scrabble Great Depression years.

Well, with the league championship on the line things were mighty tense that hot August afternoon of '32. An argument, a real rhubarb broke out in the seventh inning when an ex-major leaguer, a ringer playing for Grants Pass, reached back with his bat and smacked my Dad's catcher's mit. He squawked, "Batter interference" and danged if the local umpire didn't award him first base. The umpire was buffaloed, I suppose by the batter's major league reputation. And that sly trick forced home what turned out to be the winning run since the bases were loaded at the time.

Afterwards, Big George and Roof consoled themselves with a beer or two while eating goober peas down on the banks of the Rogue River that hot Sunday way back when.

Years later Roof was falling timber for the P.L. Company out on Yeager Creek. On a wet, slippery day while limbing a downed tree his axe glanced off a limb and bit into his calked boot.[1] As Roof told the story, he sat down in the rain, unlaced his boot, and turned it up. "That little toe came rolling out of my boot just like a goober pea!"

About fifty years later when Mabel and I were courting, we went back to Southern Oregon to see a play at Ashland. Afterward we drove out toward Prospect. Between Eagle Point and Trail I pointed out the road down to Dodge Bridge. It was the road down to my grandfather's farm where Reese Creek, you know, runs into the Rogue River. No further than one hundred yards on Mable said, "That's the house where I was born." A few miles further she showed the way up Reese Creek where she started school. Then she told me about her father who used to have a W.P.A. job on the Prospect Dam. And so we married—the romance of coincidences was overwhelming.

Wouldn't our stars have quivered, though, if only Mabel had said, "Let me tell you a story about Sunday ball, goober peas, and a pitcher that almost won the championship for Medford in the Southern Oregon League back in 1932."

[1] All the limbs have to be cut off a downed tree before it is sawn into merchantable lengths.

TINK VERSUS WHACK

No "whack" left in the game of baseball anymore. Now it's "tink" as in the tink of metal bats—I think they are all made of some kind of Taiwan tin, definitely NOT American—that kids play with today. Old time baseball bat mumbo jumbo has been lost to the game along with the sound of "whack."

Roof, Oregon Bill's dad, his mumbo jumbo was crank case oil. Yep, that's right. All winter. All winter he'd soak a Louisville Slugger in crank case oil. We're talkin fully submerged here for eight months or more. Not a particularly big bat, a 35 incher with an average barrel. But that hummer weighed a ton come June. He'd have to let it drip and dry out for another year. Only a logger swinging an axe six days a week could get that oil soaked bat around on an inside fast ball.

Another bit of baseball bat mumbo jumbo was "boning." You'd take your favorite bat, the one that rode up in the front seat of the fliver on the way to Sunday ball games while the wife and kids rode in the back seat. That one. Stick it in the oven of the wood stove to heat it and open the grain a bit. Then you'd rub the barrel of that bat real hard with a greasy ham bone or some such. Old timers claimed it would harden that surface good for another 100 feet, which might make the difference when you hit a long fly ball out at Bull Creek some Sunday with the county championship riding on every pitch.

I had my own kid mumbo jumbo about the bats I picked up on the Calapooia River bar for rock batting. Those white hard limbs left over from beaver meals were the best. Beavers cut trees, limbs, and brush off the bank, some of which floated on down the Calapooia and dried out for my rock batting. Yes, sir, you can't beat a beaver select, sun dried wand for whacking rocks outa sight over Smith's pasture.

I discovered something about the mathematical concept of infinity with my beaver select, sun dried rock bats down on the Calapooia in my youth. You see, if you pick a flat, thin, round rock, sort of like a silver dollar, and toss it so it falls flat to you and then you whack the edge real hard with your bat, why that rock sails off into orbit. I mean they flat leave this planet and zing out beyond the Milky Way. Back in '47 when I was 17 and at my rock battin prime, I hit some sailers that are still whistling out among the galaxies somewhere. My eyes, though, are gettin too old to see infinity anymore. That's a young man's game.

But I'm not surprised that funny wrinkles in the data from out there are causing the heavy thinkers—astronomers, physicists, and such—to doubt the big bang theory. I'll bet when they get their numbers straightened out they'll find some Calapooia flat rocks sailing away out there, whizzing into those black holes, and just screwing things up royally.

That's how the phrase out-of-whack got into the English language. It all started right here in Brownsville, Oregon. Well, technically, down on a river bar on the Calapooia.

Rock Batting

The subject, rock batting, is about as narrow as a rat's tail, and to most folks just about as interesting. So you yawners just move on back to the want ads.

You know, this newspaper would be a whole lot more citified if the want ads had a "personals" section. "Old gaffer panting to meet gafferette," that sort of thing. How can you be up-town if the danged newspaper doesn't have a personals column?

But that's another story. Meanwhile, slide on over there and make room for rock batting.

Oregon Bill invented rock batting down on the Calapooia River bar, June 12, 1939. Been at it off and on for fifty years. Just picked up a stick, tossed up a rock, and swoosh. Missed.

I got pretty good, though. Used to go down to that river bar and bat rocks by the hour. Got to assemblin rival bat-teams. Picked out a good lead-off bat, then a clean-up hitter, and so forth. Fought some titanic series down there. But, you know, a river bar is not as good as a gravel pit. Gravel pits are awesome places for rock batting. Gives you a regular Candlestick Stadium feeling with Willie Mays stepping in the box, game on the line. Or, I was Rocky Colavito patrolling right field for Detroit. Only Rocky didn't patrol much on that Calapooia River bar. Mainly he whacked, winning game after game with a sailer lost on the horizon.

Or I was Big Luke Easter with his bum knee playing for the old San Francisco Seals on his way down from the Cleveland Indians. Visiting San Francisco one time

I walked with my dad from Market Street clear out to Seal's Stadium. I still don't know where in the City it was. In the Mission? Portrero Hill? I don't know. But we weren't gonna take a chance on those fool trolley cars.

Anyway, we saw Big Luke hit a shot into short right field. Hit a cement wall and the ball caromed clear back to the first baseman. Like I say, it was a shot. For a minute there, Big Luke treated Seals Stadium like it was a big pool table—nine ball off the wall into the first base pocket.

Back to Rocky Colavito. Now there's a name, isn't it? Just sounds totally big league. It's a hard belly slide into second base all by itself. "Now batting here in the spacious Calapooia River Bar Stadium, ROCKY CALAVITO!"

"Rocky steps out of the box, folks. The rookie pitcher is sweating bullets. Rocky's back in the box. Rocks in the air. Whack. Games over, folks. Time for supper. Please drive home safely and we'll see you back here at the Calapooia River Bar Stadium for the next home series."

Nope. Ma knew she'd never lose me to bums like my cousin Melvin up at the pool hall. No, sir. She lost me to the river bar and rock batting.

Getting an Education

Did you ever notice how in school names are supposed to explain stuff? You know, like you ask why the grass is green and the teacher says, "photosynthesis." I mean, photosynthesis with an exclamation point. Like that's all there is to it.

"Why is grass green?"

"Photosynthesis! You unwashed, adenoidal logger whelp!

"Next question."

That's the real danger of being good at school. Your head gets so stuffed full of names of things, you think you must know something. But names of stuff don't explain diddly.

Take the name Clarence Booberneck, for example. Clarence was a rodeo bronc rider out at the Calapooia Round-up back in the 30's. Old Clarence used to spend all winter gettin ready. He'd set two posts in the ground about 8 foot apart then he'd throw a truck tire inner tube over each one. All winter he'd huff and puff building up his leg muscles by squeezing his knees together, tugging against the stretch of those two inner tubes.

Ol' Clarence came to town flat busted on the Fourth of July, 1939. Talked the sports, down at the Boomerang Saloon, into ponying up the entry fee for bronc riders at the rodeo (that's rodeeo, podner, not your la de da Row-day-oh like they use down in Eugene). The very first horse threw Clarence clean over his head, then pounded his ribs with a hoof or two. After Booberneck got his ribs taped up, they had to take up a second collection around the pool table to get Clarence out of town to follow the rodeo to the next bronc riding shoot out, which he was bound and determined to enter, busted ribs and all.

No, a name don't explain nuthin about the demons that causes men to tick.

Or, boys either. Take Festus House, for example. When Welcome Owsley and I beat him fair and square at keeps and took all his marbles, why that Festus and his gang jumped us after school and chased us clear out to Courtney Creek. Festus was heaving rocks about the size of small cannon balls that came rolling and bounding after our heels.

Nope, a name don't explain nuthin about the passions ticking away in the skulls of folk.

Or, ball players either. Take Mingo Bianci (rhymes with Bingo Bee-yankee) for instance. The best pure hitter I ever seen. Now, I didn't play against Ol' Mingo until he was 45 or so, but he could still hit doubles all day long 350 feet up the right center alley. And, if the right fielder didn't hustle, why Mingo would be standing on third. That is, until his legs gave out shortly after he turned 40 or so. The man was pure poetry with a bat—the cadence and meter of a Louisville Slugger in the hands of Mingo Bianci was a language all its own.

That is, until Mingo run up against Lee Ferguson, a wild left handed hum-baby high school pitcher I caught. Up against old Lee, I used to listen to Ol' Mingo talk to himself in Italian. Fergy would bring a little heat right up next to Mingo's adams apple. Mingo would pick himself up, dust himself off jabbering the whole time the gist of which was, "Mama mia! Why is a business man like myself (Mingo ran a little card game across the river in Wildwood where he played poker all night every Saturday then baseball on Sunday) commit suicide on a beoootiful day like this?"

No, a name don't explain nuthin about nuthin in this wonderful world of ours. So don't let schoolin get in the way of learnin about its beauty. Watchin Mingo hit one of a Sunday will put you well on the road to enlightenment. The zen of baseball, doncha know.

BLOOD
AND
FEATHERS

Welcome Owsley and Oregon Bill on the baseball diamond, 1942

Story Behind a Name

I suppose you'd like to know how Owsley got that nickname "Welcome." It happened cause he was the seventh kid born in the family. The other six were older sisters. The two sisters just before Welcome were named Faith and Hope. When Mother Owsley dropped that he-colt, why, Buckshot, the proud papa, he upped and named his brand new son "Welcome."

Welcome he was.

To be truthful, though, Buckshot actually named his son Karl Marx Owsley. "Welcome" was just a nickname to celebrate the arrival of a son in the Owsley family. Buckshot was a Wobblie, you know. Wobblies were strong in the lumber camps in Oregon and the Northwest back then. After supper in some of those lumber camp bunkhouses the talk got pretty radical during the Thirties. Men gathered around a woodstove made out of a fifty gallon drum with a door and air vent welded in on one end. Bunks were three-tiered high with wool socks and wool long johns hanging up near the ceiling. Around that stove, old timers say, was some of the fanciest symposia on Capitalism and the working stiff you'd ever wanna hear. Buckshot himself always claimed if Roosevelt hadn't brought in the progressive income tax there would have been a revolution here in the Northwest sure as shootin.

Work couldn't be found around Oregon in the Thirties. And working conditions for those who had jobs were tough. The woods boss for some outfits would ramble through the bunk house most mornings bellowing, "Roll out or roll up, you brush apes." That meant you either went to work, rain or shine, that day or you rolled up your blankets, drew your time, and headed down the tracks back to town. You were fired. Uncle Cletus, before he went up to Portland to go to work for Henry Kaiser building Liberty Ships during World War II, always said when he was a donkey puncher on a pile driver building a bridge, there were two hundred men waiting every day right there on the construction site hoping someone would get fired.

Buckshot had a hundred stories about the Wobblies. The word "sabotage," he said, came from France where militant workers there would throw wooden shoes called "Sabots" into machinery to halt factory production during labor disputes. Industrial sabotage was a hallmark of the Wobblies, or so everyone believed back then.

Up in Spokane, the Wobblies called for a general strike. Tried to shut everything down the Wobblies did. Local businessmen, industrialists, and financiers hatched up a plan to hire scabs back in Chicago. Put 'em on a train they did, and shipped two hundred or so workers out to Spokane.

Well now, every Wobblie in those days carried two items—membership cards and a little red song book. Every Wobblie could recruit and enroll new members on the spot. So when they got wind of the Chicago recruitment plan, the Wobblies infiltrated the train. When it arrived in Spokane those two hundred replacement workers marched off the train singing old timey labor songs as fully enrolled, new members of the Wobblie movement. Didn't do a lick of work in Spokane.

Up on Main Street U.S.A., there was hard feelings and a lot of fear too about them godless, red, "radical syndicalists" called Wobblies. Take the time up in Chehalis when the good folks there thought their town was going to be invaded by a boat-load of Wobblies off the skid road up in Seattle. No one knows who fired the first shot when that boat pulled up in Chehalis, but when the smoke cleared a number of Wobblies were dead and the rest of the bunch were marched off to the hoosegow.

That night the local boys were celebrating in the saloons when someone got the idea to bust into the jail. The vigilantes grabbed what they thought was a Wobblie leader. Took him out of town and hung him by the neck on the bridge over the slough. Then the whole gang went back to town to celebrate some more. The more they drank the madder they got, until they went back out to that bridge, cut down that Wobblie body and castrated him. Then they shot the body full of holes.

Yessireebob, there's quite a story about how my pal, Karl Marx "Welcome" Owsley came by his name right here in Brownsville, Oregon.

Schoolmarms

Buck hunting with Dad we'd sometimes sit on the side of a hill, look out over the country and plan our hunt so that if we jumped a deer we might run him into the other guy. Dad might say, "We'll meet at that schoolmarm over there." Now, a schoolmarm, for those of you not raised among loggers, is a term for a tree with a double crown, sort of like a teacher standing there with her pointer raised.

But then, you probably don't know what a "pointer" is either. Used to be that schooling consisted of a lot of drilling or recitation by the class with the teacher pointing line by line along a blackboard. For those drills she had a thin hickory or oak stick about three feet long with a rubber tip.

That pointer also doubled as a handy switch to whack young logger kids across the knuckles if they got way across the line of what was called "good deportment" in those days.

When Roof said we'd meet at the "schoolmarm," he meant we'd meet at the tree, often a white snag, that resembled a stern teacher, arm and pointer switch up-raised.

My dad's oldest sister, Aunt Lizzie, had been a school-marm. No, not a tree. She was a real grammar school teacher graduated from the two-year Normal School up at Monmouth. Aunt Lizzie married Uncle Percy who later became the county superintendent of schools. The neat thing about that was that she could pass along to me sample books given to Uncle Percy by salesmen. So I started to read early enough to be embarrassed when I went through the whole book pronouncing it, "Is... land" as in Robinson Carusoe's Island.

When Lizzie graduated from Normal School she took a job back in the coast range at a place called Low Gap. It was so remote she started teaching school in a tent and boarded from farmhouse to farmhouse sleeping in the spare room. School ended that year when the serious rains began.

The next year the school board built a little shingled one-room school house. She kept school all winter, riding to school on a horse, as did many of the pupils. Aunt Lizzie had one kid who regularly packed a 30-30 rifle which he carefully propped up in the corner. A mountain lion had been sighted in the area, and that kid was taking no chances. Rifle or not, the young teacher took up her pointer and drilled away.

Another schoolmarm you ought to meet was Goldy Jackson back in on Beaver Creek just south of Newport out on the coast. Miss Jackson was my fourth grade teacher, and earlier she had taught Roof, my dad.

Behind the school where Goldy taught a big, thick rope had been fastened to a big Doug Fir limb so that we could swing out over a deep gulch. It was our favorite thrill during recess. Well, I mean among fourth graders, of course. What eighth graders did for thrills at recess, especially in the spring, is another yarn.

Sure enough, Welcome Owsley swung out one day, lost his grip, dropped off into the gulch, knocking himself out just as the bell rung ending recess. Miss Jackson instructed us sternly to carry young Owsley into the school and lay him out on a table at the back of the room. Meanwhile, we started our reading circle off to the side of that big room. Pretty soon the Owsley kid come to and staggered around trying to get his bearings. Looking over her bifocals Miss Jackson ordered, "Young Owsley, get out your reader and get up here this minute. It's your turn to read."

I mean, being a schoolmarm to a passle of logger kids, you couldn't cut 'em any slack at all.

On Dangerous Brains

Met a feller the other day that had a real different way of looking at his own brain. Claimed his brain was "dangerous". Here's the yarn.

I needed someone to take my two-by-twelve cedar planks and resaw them into one-by-twelves. Took those planks up to Exotic Woods out on Highway 228 but they said their chainsaw would cut too big a kerf. Said I oughta take myself down to Cheshire and talk to George, a guy who had built hisself a little bandsaw and was milling a few logs catch-as-catch-can.

Hustled my little self down to Cheshire I did, and, was standing these with winter rains running down my neck when I began to get the drift of things. George was trying to calculate where to set the saw to slice a two-by-twelve into a one-by-twelve. He fussed. He spit. Then he began to sweat like hell even in that cold rain. First he muttered "seven sixteenths", then, it was "eleven sixteenths" and then he started using them both interchangeably. Neither measurement being right, of course.

Finally, George looks up, grins, and says, "I've got a dangerous brain, you know. Yep, the State even cancelled my driver's license, you know—said my brain was dangerous".

Come to find out he'd had an aneurysm in his skull. Surgeons entered his noggin, separated the brain stem, then reached up inside his brain and stapled a blood vessel back together. Well, that's exactly what he said, "stapled it back together." That brain stapling left George with a somewhat unpredictable body of grey matter sitting up there on top of his spine.

Nuthin strange about dangerous brains to me. Shoot, around Brownsville, I been dealing with unpredictable grey matter on top of brain stems all my natural life. Take Welcome Owsley as a prime example. One of the odd things about Welcome is the way he sneezes when he comes out into sunlight. An absolute sneezing fit. It's true. Sunshine lands on Welcome's skull and he sneezes his head off. And another thing, he's dyslexic, you know. These brain peculiarities made for a war between Welcome and most of our teachers when we were all in Grade school back in the '30s. It started with Miss Kessler in first grade.

Unbelievably fastidious, she was. Miss Kessler could take a single piece of KleenX and carefully peel so as to make two sheets out of one. I kid you not. The woman could flat out peel KleenX. Made each of those 50% KleenX sheets last a full day. We could hardly believe our eyes, Welcome and I, because when we blew our runny noses, we blasted clear through a full tissue of KleenX most of the time leaving us with a handful of snot we had to wipe clean down the pant leg of our bib overalls.

Just last Saturday night, Owsley and I were up at the Tavern, giggling our fool heads off telling Miss Kessler stories. Welcome ended things by rearing back and announcing he's figured out a long time ago how Miss Kessler got away with her Half-a-KleenX-sheet-last-all-day trick. Said it had to be that Miss Kessler never had a lick of juice in her! Not a drop. All she ever blew into that KleenX was the dry dust of her insides. That's how she did it, claims Welcome.

In those days, teachers were great for having every-body read out loud every day in the reading circle.

Every day, come hell or highwater, Miss Kessler would demand that young Owsley read a page by hisself. He'd stammer, look at that page for the longest time screwing up first his eyebrows, then his mouth. Finally he'd make a dyslexic guess turning letters sideways, upside down, reversed, and all like that there. Just screwed up royally that printed page in our reader.

Kessler would send Welcome down to the principal's office and there a kind thing would happen. That kind thing would just double Welcome's fine and pleasant war with Miss Kessler. The principal, you see, never failed to sit Owsley down and go over that exact same page out of our reader. Well, Owsley couldn't read but he could memorize stuff in a flash. Even today up at the Tavern, ol' Welcome can go on for hours reciting poems word for word. In grade school back then, you had two or three long poems to memorize in each grade—sort of aerobic, brain exercises—they thought it would do us good. Everybody forgot 'em, but not Owsley. No sir. To this day Welcome recites perfectly every Halloween, "the goblins will *get you* if you don't watch out."

Back in the classroom, Miss Kessler would take out our reader and Welcome, he'd "read " that page he'd memorized down in the principal's office. Kessler would glare at Welcome for the longest time. Then she'd mutter under her breath about "willful, nasty little boys." But, we all heard her clear as day.

Like I say, having a dangerous brain is old hat with my pal Welcome Owsley. But so far, the goblins have never got to him. Leastwise, not so's I can tell. But then, Welcome says I got what is called a plain vanilla, "safe" brain, not dangerous at all.

BLOOD AND FEATHERS

It's a wondrous world we live in that's for sure. One minute yer humming along with yer run-of-the-mill life here in Brownsville, Oregon, U.S. of A. and the next minute yer all tangled up in international, yes, even cosmic accidents. Oregon Bill got reminded of this fact over to Corvallis just last week at a little restaurant called Nearly Normals' Gonzo Cuisine.

Now, I've been eating at Normals' ever since they started out as a kind of cooperative community and opened a little hole-in-the-wall eatery over on Harrison Street, I believe it was. Always have favored their bean burrito. Yer plain Normals' burrito comes in yer basic pinto or yer fancy black bean flavors. I leave the black beans to the la-de-da professors and stick with them pintos cause they set better in the belly after you heap on the salsa and chow down.

The reason I was eating at Normals' was on account of I was looking to sell Barbara-The-Cook some of my hazelnuts to use in her hot cakes, cookies and such. You see them jakes over in Turkey up and grew 150% this year of what the world eats of hazelnuts. Faced with a glut on the world market, the Oregon Filbert Growers Bargaining Association settled for about 25 cents a pound to the grower this year. Since it costs about 30 cents to grow a pound of nuts, that quarter didn't look so hot. So I had several tons of my hazelnuts cracked out. Mable and I have been hand sorting them at the kitchen table this winter and peddling nut meats catch as catch can.

Funny, ain't it, having your little two by four, down home, Mable and Bill nut business jerked around by, I suppose, ordinary enough souls trying to make a living way off over there in Turkey? I mean we're talking Istanbul here! Sounds remote and exotic, don't it? Tain't so.

Eating at Normals' always reminds me of my pal Welcome Owsley who on most days you might say was nearly normal hisself. But looks are deceiving. Take the time your Welcome got hisself tangled up with that gypsy woman. Those high jinx turned out to have a cosmic twist to boot. Here's the yarn.

You know how sweet and balmy the air has been here in Brownsville these first weeks in March? Sort of intoxicating, ain't it? Well, back in the '40s Welcome he got drunk on just that kind of a late spring and swears to this day that somehow he got bonked on the head by the Little Dipper! You know how the Dipper looks like a frying pan hanging low on the night horizon. Well, Welcome Owsley swears it whanged him on the head the night he ran away with the carnival after the Pioneer Picnic in what should have been his junior year in high school.

It was that gypsy woman and her gin kisses, claims Welcome, that caused that starry frying pan whang on the head. The woman actually was from England, but as a youngster her family joined a caravan in Europe every spring and traveled casually with a band of gypsies all summer, returning to England just before Thanksgiving. When they got back the whole family got a few weeks work slaughtering turkeys. That gypsy woman claimed there was nothing better for getting you in the holiday mood than a cloud of feathers floating all about to land and stick in random puddles of blood. I mean she was an odd one that carnival gypsy woman.

She taught Welcome the finer points of the gin kiss. Sip a little gin that gypsy woman would, and then plant a good one on Welcome's lips sharing a little of the gin to boot. It was intoxicating enough that the Little Dipper whanged Welcome on the noggin that early summer of '48.

The spell lasted until late October of that year and wasn't broken until they reached Astoria where the autumn rains ended the carnival season. "Besides," says Welcome, "all the gypsy could talk about was blood and turkey feathers." So Welcome, he came on back home.

He's never been quite right since, though there are times when you'd swear he was nearly normal.

TOWN RAKE

Welcome Owsley, like I say, is Brownsville's only certified town rake. But recently a few greenhorns have raised some doubts about Ol' Welcome's credentials. So I've decided to go public. His record speaks for itself.

One of the best yarns folks remember about Welcome Owsley is the time his wife jumped him about stayin out all night ramblin and carryin on down at the Boomerang Saloon or who knows where.

"Slept all night on the hammock," says Welcome. Then, warming righteously to the thought of how he'd been wronged, he added, "I was right here at home sound asleep in the hammock before the chickens got on their roost!"

"Welcome Owsley, you rascal," shot back his wife, "I took that hammock down two weeks ago!"

But Ol' Welcome, he doesn't miss a beat. He looks her right in the eye and sez, "Well, that's my story and I'm stickin to it!"

For years after that whenever a Brownsville husband got in a fix with his wife he'd rear back, grin and bellow, "Well, that's my story and I'm stickin to it!"

But if the truth be known, Welcome's one and only political caper first established him as our true town rake. Separated him from mere bounders and common drunks.

Actually, politics was forced on Welcome by the town fathers back when the Boomerang Saloon was a lusty institution and favored mightily by Welcome and his social set. Seems like the town fathers in a moment of indiscretion reared up on their hind legs and passed an ordinance that said no saloon shall be nearer than three hundred feet from a church.

Well now, you can imagine how that news agitated the Boomerang regulars since that fine and venerable institution sat practically cheek by jowl with one of the more vigorous old time churches in town. I mean the boys were getting themselves pretty worked up when Welcome hisself walks through the swinging doors with that lopsided, droll grin hanging on his mug. The boys practically busted a gut telling him the news about the ordinance and its probable effects on their fine social club.

"Yes sir boys, I heard the news and I think its a mighty fine ordinance. It demands our strongest efforts to enforce it," announces Welcome to the whole room.

It was Snoose Svenson who recovered first. Snoose, he hobbled up front on that badly bent leg of his that he'd busted years ago when his climbing spikes caught as he was high balling it to beat hell down that spar pole way back up Courtney Creek and asked, "eh?"

"Have to move that blamed church," says Welcome. "Yep, citizen's initiative is a fine old Oregon tradition. We're goin to get us a citizen's initiative petition requiring them to move the church and bring it into compliance with our fine new ordinance."

You should have seen the grins spread around that room down at the Boomerang Saloon on that rainy Sunday back there in the middle of the Great Depression. And I'll be blamed if the humor of it all wasn't catching. Seems like everyone around town stepped up, giggled a bit, then signed Welcome's initiative petition.

At their very next meeting the town fathers quietly moved to table the motion for the three-hundred-foot ordinance. Several of the town fathers then adjourned to the back room down at the Boomerang. And the uneasy peace between church and saloon continued until the Boomerang burned down a few years later.

Well, that's my yarn and I'm stickin to it.

DOMESTIC TRANQUILITY

My pal Welcome Owsley claims few things are harder to put up with than a good example. I think that's why we've been life-long friends—the danger of setting a good example has not been very strong. In fact you might say it was remote, especially in the matter of domestic tranquility.

Take the time Welcome decided to oil his roof for winter. This happened sometime ago when they used to save up crank case oil to daub on dry shingles. Welcome bought a little powered graphite to mix with the crank case oil, then got a broom and set to sweeping on the oil from a five-gallon bucket.

Well, things got a mite slippery so ol' Welcome, he come down and got himself a long rope. He heaved one end up over the peak of the roof and then looked around for something solid to tie the other end to. Not a tree or a stump or a fence post was close enough to the house to give him the right amount of play in the end of the rope thrown over the roof top. So Welcome backed his pickup just the right distance from the house. After he tied his rope good and solid, he got back up on the roof, tied the end of the rope around his waist and set to swabbing that slippery roof in serene confidence.

Not more than fifteen minutes later Minnie, Welcome's wife, comes charging out of the house, jumps in the pick up, and tears off down the driveway!

She's on her way to town. Welcome's on his way up over the roof and down the other side. Minnie only drug him about seventy-five feet before the yelling and cussing brought her to a stop.

In the emergency room while they set Welcome's leg, Minnie swore up and down she never saw the rope tied to the bumper of that truck. But, you know, Welcome cuts a pretty wide swath down at the Boomerang Saloon and elsewhere. I always wondered how Minnie put up with it. And from the hard, bright look in her eye I think I know the answer.

Minnie cinched it when she looked at Welcome in that hospital bed and quoted one of his very own favorite sayings. She said, "You know dear, you can't tell how good a man or a watermelon is until you thump 'em."

Welcome got to do some thumpin of his own later. It happened when he reported to the County Sheriff that Minnie was a missing person. She hadn't been home for two days. Well the Sheriff he starts checking around and he finds her in about two hours. In fact he calls on Minnie and asks her why she's a missing person. And this makes her mad as hell. "I ain't no missing person," she says, "Welcome hisself checked me into this hospital not two days ago! Just wait 'til I get outa here!"

The way Welcome and I figure it, domestic tranquility is an oxymoron.

Using a four-bit word like "oxymoron" called for a little libation down at the Boomerang Saloon. Pretty soon we were pounding the table, giggling, and telling stories on each other. Which led me to ask my pal why we were all the time doin such dumb stuff. And old Welcome sez, "Bill, the good citizens of Brownsville should be thankful to have us around. Without fools like us, most folks wouldn't amount to a tinker's damn."

By a Nose

My pal, Welcome Owsley, could pass for normal, I think, if he'd just read ordinary stuff like Louis L'Amour, Readers' Digest, or the AARP Bulletin. You know, regular stuff. But not ol' Welcome. No, sir. Weird books stick to Welcome like peanut butter to the top of your mouth.

Now he's gotten aholt of a book called, *The Science of Breath*. Trust Welcome Owsley to take a shine to some pointy-headed professor trying to make something fancy out of a subject as down-home, cut-and-dried, as plain ordinary as breathing. He's all the time jabbering about one cockamamie idea or another from his new book. Just the other day we got a mess of dirty looks from the afternoon regulars up on the highway at the Calapooia Drive-In when ol' Welcome, he up and asks real loud, "Bill, do you know why snot doesn't just run out of your nose?" Well, let me tell you that four o'clock coffee crowd raised an eyebrow or two at Welcome's question, you betcha. They weren't all that interested either when Welcome explained about all these little hairs that pulsate in a wave motion back up the inner passages of the old shnozzola. Called those snot carrying hairs "cilia," Welcome did.

I thought it was pretty damned "cilia" myself.

But by this time Welcome had the bit in his teeth and couldn't be reined in. All I could do was hang on for a full conversational gallop about his new book, particularly the chapter on "Nasal Functioning and Energy." That crazy Owsley says there is erectile tissue in three, not two, places on the body. We all know about the first two, of course, but Welcome swears the third place is inside the nose. Says there's a well documented medical syndrome called "Honeymooner's Nose." Seems like newly married couples, carrying on like newly married couples are likely to do, sometimes develop a chronically engorged lining of the nose. It's a kinda sympathetic interaction of different regions of the body. Stimulation of body parts one and two arouse the lining of body part three, the shnozzola.

Now, Welcome sez, he understands the Eskimo kiss—rubbing noses. Sez he understands too why Charles Boyer and all those other suave Frenchmen talk through their noses—"Chronically engorged lining" gives 'em dead away every time.

So inspired was Welcome, he went out and rented himself a pink gorilla suit. The occasion was Minnie's sixtieth birthday. Before Minnie woke up on her sixtieth birthday morning old Welcome slips out and puts on his pink gorilla outfit. He comes bounding and grunting back into the room, hops up on the bed and asks, "Is it true old ladies still like to monkey around?"

Minnie? She's still shrieking.

Ol' Welcome says he got to thinking about the wide flaring nostrils of the gorilla. Said he couldn't resist putting the chapter on "Nasal Functioning and Energy" to a real life test right here in Brownsville, Oregon.

LET YER EARS HANG DOWN

Will and Rosy (William Robert and Rosa Emmamarine),
the young couple given a gentle charivari by friends and
family following their marriage, 1895

TALKING WITH DEAD KIN

Just relax and unlax there. Ease back and don't get uptight.

We'll take this topic—how to talk with folks that are dead—real calm and sober like. I don't understand all I know about this stuff, you see. I'm just reporting what happened to Oregon Bill.

I learned to visit with dead kin by accident when I was buck hunting one time. All I was doing was pussy-footing[1] down an open oaks ridge deep in the golden grass when it happened.

Because it was dry country in the coast hills way south of here and this ridge was well away from water at the windmill, the range cattle couldn't get to the feed and so the grass grew knee high. This time of the year it lay yellow under the oaks. Well, I was moseying along real slow pretending I was Uncle Cletus or Uncle Merlyn, both of whom would hunt barefoot for short spells in good deer country when conditions were dry and snappy underfoot.

Way down the ridge ahead of me I saw horns lift up suddenly out of the dry grass. I raised the rifle—a .32 special with an old-fashioned octagonal barrel, and sighted down the open buckhorn sights. That's what made it so perfect. Not only was the afternoon sun slanting through the oaks, not only had I hunted well enough to catch a buck in his bed, but I was packing my grandfather's

---

[1] To "pussy-foot" is to walk as quietly as a cat; also connotes being circumspect and unobtrusive.

rifle. I touched her off, and, bang! I blinked as three deer, poof, disappeared off the end of the ridge in one jump.

Slipping on down the ridge I got caught up in the perfection of this world. Surprised and yet not surprised, I found that buck still in his bed, neck broken by a shot that had caught him under the chin, severing his spine instantly. It was just too righteous.

Hunkering down on my heels I pondered the oaks, the grass, the shot, and the autumn light on the blue of that buck's coat. Just then Roof, my dad, came up, hunkered down on his heels too, and commenced to roll a Bull Durham cigarette. A swipe of the tongue sealed the paper. He twisted the ends and lit up the smoke, which was his habit either when he got his buck or when he had wounded one in the brush and wanted to give it time to lay up and get stiff before he started tracking it.

We exchanged a few congratulatory words, but mostly we just sat there on our heels in the sweet grass. After a while my hunting partner gave a holler from the next ridge over. I turned, and Dad was gone. Which, I guess, was a necessary thing to do since he had been killed when a tree gave way in the deep mud and wet rain out in Yeager Creek three years before.

Like I say, it was all an accident, but it taught me to look out for moments when you can have a smoke and a chat with folks that are dead. That's why I'm learning how to drive a horse to harness. I'd like to visit just a little with William Ridge, my great grandfather and a teamster.

Which brings me around to Tennessee Tucker, Ridge's wife and my great grandmother. I'd give a bushel of turnips to talk with that lady.

I'd like to ask her if it's true that when she balked at the sight of the Cascade Mountain, ol' Ridge strapped a thumb-back chair onto the side of a mule, roped Tennessee onto the chair, and hauled her over the Santiam Pass down into Brownsville. I've got that rawhide bottom chair over at my place. Every once in a while I sit myself down on it. But no Tennessee. It's one of those things where goin at it directly doesn't ever work.

Another thing, I'd like to ask Tennessee about her milking. That woman loved her buttermilk and had to have milk cows around the place all the time. Now Ridge was a Southern gentleman who had met Tennessee on a wagon train coming west from Arkansas after the Civil War. After a short, travelling courtship they were married beside an unknown stream in Texas. Southern gentlemen are gallant enough but have some definite ideas about what kind of work they will do. So after the birth of one more child, there were nine, Ridge would tether the milk cow at the back door. Then he'd carry Tennessee out from her bed and set her on the milk stool. Ever so thoughtfully he'd hold a parasol to protect Tennessee from the rain while she milked that cow and got her buttermilk.

Well, wouldn't you want to talk to that woman? I know she'd be tickled that her great-grandson got named after a state too. Oregon Bill meets Tennessee Tucker. It's gonna happen, but sorta sideways, not straight on and planned out.

Let Yer Ears Hang Down

My pal Welcome Owsley says you oughta let yer ears hang down and listen good when an old hand is talkin. Course, Welcome also claims old timers are folks who've had a lot of experiences—some of them are even true.

So back your buns up to the wood stove there. Grab yourself a cup of java and let yer ears hang down while I tell you about Rosy and Will and their gentle charivari (pronounced, "shiv-ah-ree").

You don't know what a charivari is? Well, damn. Taught you everything I know and you still don't know anything.

A charivari is a lot of whooping and hollering, maybe even a few gunshots and other highjinxs, carried on around the lodgings of a young couple on their wedding night. In horse and buggy days a honeymoon was unheard of among common folk. So a young couple spent their wedding night right among their kin. In case the young didn't realize what a special night it was, why everyone gathered around to carry on a bit. You could count on some rascally uncle getting liquored up and going a little too far. Things might even get a little physical outside the bedroom when one of the patriarchs would bellow, "That's enough boys."

The other day Ma showed me the newspaper clipping from the *Brownsville Times*, March 17, 1895, for Will and Rosy, my grandfather and grandmother. The clipping speaks of a "gentle charivari." Here are some excerpts.

"The happy couple started for the valley in carriages. Arriving at the residence of J.D. Cobb, father of the bride, the newly wedded couple were met by a host of relatives and friends who gladly welcomed them. At 5 o'clock p.m. supper was served at which the gathering enjoyed such a variety of dainties as are seldom...," and here a tear in the newspaper clipping makes the next line illegible. But it goes on to report, "and gave Rosy and Will a gentle charivari and were treated to cake, lemonade, cigars, and singing, and kept things interesting until the short hours of the next day."

"Lemonade, cigars, and singing." Isn't that great? A "gentle charivari." Bunch of us ought to whomp up a reenactment over at the Moyer House and Museum sometime this spring. Ol' Bill will personally watch the lemonade to make sure Welcome Owsley doesn't spike it—with too heavy a hand.

About 15 years later, Will was killed when a limb fell and struck him one night after work out on the right-of-way for the 101 highway down on the coast. Left Rosy with seven children.

My mother tells me Rosy was an expert seamstress. Seems like she took in sewing to help make ends meet. She would take old suits apart, turn them inside out, then sew back together a "new" suit for the paying customer.

See, it pays to follow ol' Welcome's advice—hang down yer ears and listen when old folks speaks. I'm sure right now you've got a big itch to take your needle and turn all them old suits inside out right this minute.

No sir, the throwaway society isn't so new after all. But, time was when things were broke down, played out, used up, and threadbare before they was throwed away.

Right here in Brownsville, Oregon, U.S.A.

BUDDIES

Right next to the grave of Tennessee Tucker is the grave of Goody Barnwell. Tennessee and Goody crossed the Cascade Mountains together riding double on the back of a mule one fine spring morning in 1871. Old Grannie Sweazy told my mother the yarn and I'll pass it along.

The story starts in Fordyce, Arkansas where William Ridge, my great grandfather, married one of the Jones girls—Mary Catherine—in 1848. The young couple, now blessed with two children, joined a wagon train bound for California in 1855. Sometime later in the Humboldt Basin, in what is now Nevada, the wagon train made camp. Ridge went ahead to scout a camp for the next day. While he was gone, Indians over ran the camp. Mary Catherine hid in the brush with the two babies, Rufus Ridge and Nancy. Late that night she ran. They found Mary Catherine unconscious later, and both babies were still alive.

Ridge turned around and headed home. Mary Catherine and Nancy died of pneumonia on the way back to Arkansas.

Father and son stayed in Fordyce for just a short while before deciding to come west again. On that second wagon train west, Ridge met and married Tennessee Tucker. They were hitched in Texas by the banks of some unnamed river.

Also on that wagon train was a young girl named Goody Barnwell. Goody sort of adopted Tennessee as older sister and they grew to become life-long friends.

The Barnwells and Oregon Bill's kin both came over

the Santiam Pass in the Cascade Mountains together. Granny Sweazy reported to my mother that when they made it to Brownsville, Tennessee Tucker and Goody Barnwell were riding back-to-back on the same mule waving to one and all as they forded the Calapooia River and rode through town.

The Barnwell family settled out in Thief's Neck Country near Strong's Station. But Goody and Tennessee got together whenever they could and most especially fell on each others neck[1] when they came to the Pioneer Picnic every June.

Years later when Tennessee died, the Barnwell family bought the cemetery plot right next to her grave. Goody Barnwell was eventually buried in that plot beside her life-long friend.

And Rufus Ridge? He died of cirrhosis of the liver, I believe. Where he's buried no one knows.

---

[1] I first heard "fall on their neck" from my Aunt Ruby who used the phrase as a wry description of the exuberant hugs in family greetings.

Priorities

How do you say "YES" to life? Say "YES" every time and not get caught up in the petty distractions? It's a tough nut to crack and Oregon Bill wanders around lost a good bit of the time just like you do. But, recalling a couple of family yarns helps him to find his path again. The first story starts at the Boomerang Saloon in old-time Brownsville; the second story begins in Southern Oregon down on his grandfather's farm near Dodge Bridge out Sam's Valley way down on the Rogue River.

Back before the flood of '09, the sports around the pool table in Brownsville were remarkably clear about priorities. William Ridge, Bill's great-grandpop, was hangin out at the Boomerang Saloon, a rough and ready outfit just east of town, when someone got the idea, "Let's all go huntin!" Before you know it they had passed the hat, loaded old Ridge up in the buckboard, and sent him off to the Brown and Blakley store to get supplies. Everyone else hightailed it for home to grab a rifle and other necessaries.

Hunting back then was a premier social occasion; male bonding in its finest hour, you might say.

Those bonds came unstuck in a hurry though when Ridge pulled up in front of the Boomerang all loaded and rarin' to go. The boys took a gander under the tarp and immediately demanded an accounting.

"What do you ribbon clerks mean, "an accounting"? Anybody can plainly see I got $40 in supplies—$5 in grub and $35 in whiskey."

"We can all see that, you old fool," yelled Idus Owsley. "Why did you buy so damned many groceries?"

All the boys down at the Boomerang Saloon agreed

that William Ridge had lost track of priorities. "We're not holdin no dinner party; we're goin huntin," snorted Snoose Svenson that Saturday early in the autumn way back when Brownsville was a pup.

The second yarn about priorities is a knee slapper that Bill's maternal grandfather loved to tell about the hired hand.

Grandpa Haight hired this hand to work on his farm outside Eagle Point in Southern Oregon. But no sooner had the hay been put up loose in the barn than that hand told Grandpa Haight he was quittin.

"Well, I sort of figured that," said Grandpa. "It was getting up at 4:30 a.m. to work before breakfast, wasn't it?"

"Nope, wasn't that," said the hand.

"Well then, that 15 minute lunch out in the field got to ya, huh?"

"Nope."

"You didn't like workin 'til 8 every night, I'll bet."

"Nope. Didn't mind that either," said the hand.

"Well, all I can think it might be was sittin around doin hand work, shellin peas and such, by lamp light a couple hours after dinner," said Grandpa Haight.

"Nope, not that either."

"Well, what in tarnation is it, man? Why you quittin me?"

"When I hired on here you promised me a full-time job, and I don't do a lick from midnight 'til four in the morning," replies the hand.

Grandpa would slap his knee when he came to the punch-line of that story, cross my heart. It's a gesture you don't see anymore. But it's a message about priorities sly old gaffers have been telling since the first grandson looked up in rapt attention at his grandpop.

WEARING O' THE CAPE

This is a salute. So all you pilgrims stop slurping your morning coffee and stand up straight there. Bring your arm up smartly, hand at the eye brow. Hold it for 3 seconds or so then return it briskly to your side. Good. Its proper we should think of Lizzie, Oregon Bill's auntie, every now and again. Here's the yarn.

In the '40s there were only three people in the whole world, at least in my world, that wore a full length, dark blue cape—Franklin Delano Roosevelt, General Chang Kaishek, and my Aunt Lizzie. I don't know why those other birds stood around covered in all that good cloth, but my Aunt's reason was practical—perfect strangers didn't need to know about the loss of her arm and breast to cancer surgery.

Did everything, that woman. Raised three kids doing all her own washing as well as ironing. Now, Oregon Bill is pretty handy with an iron but to this day I don't know how she smoothed every wrinkle, say in the yoke of a shirt, or steamed those arrow-straight creases in the trousers of her boys and Uncle Percy. And this was long before wash-and-wear clothes.

Goin to Aunt Lizzie's was like stepping into a Norman Rockwell painting right there on the *Saturday Evening Post* magazine. I mean that family had a big collie better than Lassie herself or himself, I forget which. Her son Bill, the one who got killed in the Aleutian Islands up in Alaska early in WW II, was an eagle scout who, with his brother Dick, had neat, neat model airplanes they designed themselves, steam engine experiments, and stuff like that they'd show you. And on the back lawn was a hammock to swing in.

Out near Cobb's store beyond Low Gap, Uncle Percy and Aunt Lizzie had a permanent summer camp set up. I got to go there for a couple of weeks most summers. Aunt Lizzie cooked all the meals at a big wood range they had set up outdoors under a tarp. After breakfast we'd play pinecone baseball.

I better take a minute here to tell you that pinecone baseball was invented by Oregon Bill, July 8, 1941 out at Low Gap. The game is played with sticks for bats and pine cones for balls. It's a two-person game, a pitcher and a hitter, where you designate which hits will be singles, doubles, and so on. Oregon Bill was at one time a premier player and is the holder of several medals from the Pine Cone Baseball Olympics. He only appears now at old timer games and other ceremonial family occasions and has trouble handling the young rookies and "phenoms" coming up.

But back to the yarn about Lizzie's camp.

Later when it would get hot, we'd all dive for white rocks at the swimming hole. Then we'd work crossword puzzles, play Chinese checkers, stuff like that. At night we'd try to shoot swooping, diving bats with BB guns as we waited for the evening campfire and sing-a-long. It was just a straight-out kid heaven.

But probably my sharpest memory is of the Christmas tree at Aunt Lizzie's one year. They lived then out in the middle of the Willamette Valley where Uncle Percy was the principal of a small grammar school. The family rented a big Victorian house with tons of gingerbread, stairs, attics, and closets, just perfect for hide-and-seek and stuff like that.

Like I say, this particular Christmas the most wonderfilled event was the tree itself. We were ushered into the parlor late in the evening on Christmas Eve. There in the room was a nice but pretty ordinarily decorated tree. The lights were turned out. A match was struck and candles on the tree were lit one by one. And we all came to know that the candles illuminated not just the tree but our souls as well. Within the hold of that candle light Aunt Lizzie led us in singing a carol or two. Then the candles were put out. But long after, the wonder of a candlelit tree stayed in our hearts.

I have my own long, blue cape now just like FDR, Generalissimo Chang, and my Aunt Lizzie. So if you see me down at the General Store some winter day all decked out in my long blue, try not to snort or snicker. The occasion will be pretty cosmic, you see. Oregon Bill will be walking with his Aunt Lizzie.

THE $700 HOUSE

Uncle Cletus died last month in the house he had lived in his entire adult life. The house was given to him; it cost $700 whole dollars.

Here's the yarn.

Back when hay was mowed, shocked, and put up loose in the barn the work was hard, the hours long, and the horses sometimes balky. Turns out young Cletus was long on work and good with horses.

He must have been a crackerjack hand because one day the owner of the place where Cletus worked asked, "Is it true yer gettin yourself married, Clete?"

Cletus allowed as how it was probably true.

"Married man ought to have a house for his bride. Here is the key to that Jones place up on Church Street," he continued. "It's yours. Pay me back the $700 when you get around to it."

Like I say, Uncle Cletus died in that house last Spring sixty years or so after it was given to him to make him a real married man. Seems quaint don't it to remember a time when loyalty between boss and hired hand ran deep and ran both ways.

But then Uncle Cletus was born in the wrong century doncha know. Yep. Should have been born a mountain man in the fur trade of the early 1800's. He was pretty much aware of God's blunder but waded through the 20th century with a lopsided grin on his mug. Said he always figured the Lord was a little bored and needed him, Cletus as a sort of cosmic joke good for a giggle every once in awhile.

Cletus started working in hay fields damned near

as soon as he could walk or so it seemed. Worked for his grandfather J.D. Cobb. Use to tell of the time he was loading hay up on top of the wagon while J.D. and another hand pitched hay up to him. One of the two pitched up a shock of hay. Up came the hay on the end of the pitch fork along with a rattlesnake.

"I could hear the snake buzzing away and feel it thrashing around in the hay up against my legs," said Cletus. "So over backwards I went landing on the wagon tongue between the horses."

"Well, when a kid comes flying out of the sky, you just know those horses are going to bolt," continued Cletus. "When I came to I found my arm broke, bone sticking out in two places. They took me to town in the Model T. Doc Wells set the arm and told me to come back in three months when he'd remove the cast."

Not more than a month later, Cletus took a ball peen hammer and cracked off that itchy cast. His mother caught him and marched him back to the doctor's office.

"Ol' Doc Wells, hummed a little bit and muttered something about it not healing right," continued Uncle Cletus," and then said, "close your eyes boy."

"Well, he had me by the elbow with both hands and pounded that elbow over the corner of the operating table to break it all over again."

"The only pain killer he gave me was, "close your eyes boy!"

"I kicked that sawbones right in the belly. My fool elbow never did work right after that."

No sir, Uncle Cletus was not what you'd call the prototype twentieth century man. But there he was doin the best he could with this little slice of time, this small wedge of space in the world he was born to.

The $350 House

I guess everywhere in Oregon they've had the experience of some Jasper from California paying big bucks for a place and then the County Assessor comes round and ups the assessed valuation of all the property in the neighborhood. And you get socked with higher taxes.

Raises hell with the blood pressure don't it? And that just leads to another expense—getting the Doc to fiddle with your prescription.

But what folks don't know is Californians been doin it to each other down there for a long time. Take my Uncle Art and Aunt Ilah for instance. They both worked in the logging mill for the P.L. Company down in Rohnerville back in the 30's. Saved up a whole wad of dough and bought themselves a home. Paid cash. Three hundred and fifty dollars, got 'em a clear title. And they settled in cozy as could be.

Things were just swell until Cletus, Ilah's brother, bought the place next door. Actually, his boss, a ranch owner, bought it for him cause Cletus was gettin married and his boss being an old fashioned sort thought a married man ought to have a threshold to carry his bride across. Paid $700 for that threshold.

Sure enough the County Assessor got wind of those high prices and doubled Art's taxes on the spot. I don't think Art's blood pressure ever returned to normal after that. You see down at the mill, Art whacked up his back real bad late in those Great Depression years. Spent the rest of his life in a wheel chair, only able to sort of slide out of the chair once in awhile and crawl out to weed the garden or some such.

Aunt Ilah returned to work over at P.L. after Art got hurt just as the war was coming on. The family got by mainly because they owned their house free and clear. And Ilah worked at all sorts of jobs.

She was even a sheriff for awhile. Well, she wasn't actually the County Sheriff like we kids thought but she did work at the jail booking prisoners and things. The family never had it so good; our outlaw kin now had one of their own with the keys to the county jug. Ilah had a big badge, a gun, a snazzy hat and everything. So all us kids thought she was just as good as the sheriff of the county.

But Ilah didn't start out to be a police officer. You see, these were the war years of the 40's. and Ilah hooked on as a kind of "Rosy the Riveter" for Henry Kaiser, building Liberty Ships in the local ship yards. She went to school and ended up running an acetylene torch until a cousin of ours, Albert Nichols, who really was a sheriff, hired Ilah to work for him.

Work was Ilah's middle name. I learned about this the time I dropped in on her when she was fifty something. I asked what was new and she said, "Oh, I've been reviewing my shorthand. You never know when a new job will pop up." Those notes she was reviewing were from her high school days more than thirty years earlier. She was still keeping those skills polished!

Now, the reason I dropped in on Ilah to catch her reviewing her high school shorthand was because I was newly single after twenty-seven years of married life. I was lonesome for family, and I thought the chances were pretty good that I could chat a spell and with any luck cage a piece of Ilah's wild blackberry pie. Ilah had even offered to teach me how to whomp up a pie by myself. It's a lesson I'll never forget.

"Bill," she sez right off, "you have to learn to play. The whole secret to pie-dough is to get downright playful. If you take pie-dough seriously, it will stick and fuss up on you every time. So just play."

With that she took the big Orange Crush bottle she used as a rolling pin and rolled out that pie dough just as pretty as you please. Made me a wild black-berry pie on the spot.

It was just the advice a lonesome bachelor needed. I've found since then that if you take life seriously it will "stick and fuss up on you every time."

So, just play!

THE $8 DOLLAR HOUSE

Oregon Bill's brother Jumpy calls his home the Eight Dollar House. That's 'cause he paid just eight whole dollars for the place.

Here's the yarn.

Actually, Jumpy had to pony up a regular down payment for the house. But naturally he didn't have that kind of cash laying around, so he hit up everyone he knew. Got a loan right off from his boss out at the oil patch. Even put the touch on his ex-wives. And I'll be damned if one of them didn't come through and give him better than a thousand dollars.

One way or another ol' Jumpy got the down payment scrabbled together and waltzed into the savings and loan office to close the deal. After all the charges were totaled up Jumpy could see he was short. He was light by a measly eight dollars and didn't have another thin dime in his pockets.

Jumpy already had borrowed from every relative, friend, acquaintance, lover, past lover, and ex-wife he could think of. No way he could pick up a phone and get that eight dollars. Didn't qualify for plastic, so that was out too. The sad truth was he'd put on the table every damn red cent he had. And Jumpy was divorced so he couldn't even sneak in and shake down one of the kid's piggy banks.

Jumpy, he reared back and looked at the savings and loan officer across the table. The savings and loan type looked right back not giving an inch.

"Count that poke one more time, mister," says Jumpy. "Be right back."

Busted right out the door and onto the street. Sashayed up to the very first stranger he saw coming down the street and explained his situation. That's Jumpy. Been that way his whole life. Got a heart as big as all outdoors and everybody just naturally takes a shine to him.

Wouldn't you know that stranger sprung for the eight dollars. Jumpy hustled back in to close the deal and that's why he's always called his place the Eight Dollar House.

Jumpy his ownself takes a shine to folks too, especially folks that have been whipsawed by life. Take the time Jumpy met Mother Trucker down at the local tavern. Mother Trucker had a sad story to tell and before you know it ol' Jumpy sez, "Why hell, Mother Trucker, you just move into the Eight Dollar House til you can get on your feet. Shoot, I'm roughnecking in the oil patch and I ain't never home."

Mother Trucker did just that, promising Jumpy she'd pay a little rent out of her welfare check. But doncha know the welfare check hardly covered Mother Trucker's social obligations down at the tavern where she and Jumpy met.

Come Spring who should show up at the door of the Eight Dollar House but Mother Trucker's pregnant daughter and grandchildren. Jumpy couldn't say "no" to them either and so that whole passel moved in too. But things looked rosy cause the daughter said her welfare check could help a little with the rent too.

Not more than a month later a scruffy, adenoidal type showed up at the door saying he was the probable poppa for Mother Trucker's daughter's impending child. So he moved in too. Didn't have no welfare, but that didn't make much difference to Jumpy cause he was workin steady and rent is rent no matter how many folks are under the roof.

About that time, though, I got hot under the collar and I sez to my brother, "Jumpy, the government might not like you goin into the welfare business. The government doesn't like competition. You look out, you hear?"

'Ol Jumpy? He just grinned.

He'd be out at the oil patch roughnecking weeks at a time. This made for some hard adjustments because Mother Trucker's crew would settle into a nice routine at the Eight Dollar House entertaining, partying, having friends stay over and such. Jumpy coming home put the damper on things and they sure let him know. Got to be such a hassle for Jumpy he got to sleeping over in the well driller's shack out at the oil patch.

Jumpy was ready for divorce and he wasn't even married.

But wouldn't you know, the Universe solved Jumpy's problem real nice. Yep. Jumpy came home one night to find the Eight Dollar House surrounded by the cops. Flashing lights everywhere. Looked like a regular SWAT team in action. Turns out Mother Trucker dealt a few drugs just to sort of supplement the welfare check.

Eight Dollar House is mighty quiet lately. Jumpy? Why he's feeling kinda lonesome. Tells me he's struck up a conversation with Big Betty down at the tavern.

AMAZING GRACE

Buckshot Owsley (Welcome's Dad), Grandpa Haight,
and William Rufus, (left to right), 1938

Suckin' Hind Tit

There's just no way the runt of any pig litter can shoulder other piglets out of the way and shove his way up to mama's belly and glom onto the fattest, juiciest teat just dripping with milk. Nope. Life has dealt him another hand. He has to get by sucking hind tit, that dried-up skinny one at the end of the row.

When I was 10 years old I got to pack my first and only coffin, a four-foot wooden box containing the runty body of the kid next door. Now there was a kid that sucked life's hind tit. Truly.

The next door kid was the son of a scaler for the P.L. Company by the name of Shorty Maddox. Shorty and my dad, Roof, had a neighborly enough relationship in a standoffish sort of way. Dad was a faller in the woods, doncha know, and fallers just naturally don't get along with scalers. You see, a scaler is a company man that measures up the timber a faller puts down and bucks up into merchantable logs. Scalers are pretty well known for pulling the tape in favor of the company or "losing" a log or two in the week's scale and therefore shorting the faller's pay.

Another thing that rubbed Roof the wrong way was the fact Shorty was a relatively young man. In Roof's eyes Shorty was taking a job away from an old stove-up logger. Used to be that fallers too banged up or too old to cut the mustard were pensioned off as scalers by the company. After WW II that all changed and the P.L. began hiring young men in the woods as scalers. That and the development of the modern chainsaw meant falling timber was becoming a young man's game, and this worried the hell out of the old timers still in the woods.

Us kids called Shorty's son "Puny" in that innocently cruel way children have. Puny was a runty little sugar diabetic. And Puny's disease was serious enough that he was absolutely forbidden to have any candy whatsoever. The danger was so real that Shorty and his wife toured the two grocery stores and the one candy shop in town regularly to warn the clerks not to sell Puny any candy.

Sure enough Puny got aholt of a nickel or a dime one day, and found a clerk new to the job who would sell him candy. He went off to eat it in secret.

When Puny was found his coma was so deep they couldn't bring him around. Puny had found his sugar tit at last and it killed him. And that's how I got to be a pall bearer at age ten. Fifteen cents worth of candy did it, doncha know.

I was talkin with my pal Welcome Owsley the other day reminiscing about putting poor Puny into the ground that June way back then. Welcome said he'd been thinking about how we carried Puny's coffin and he'd started looking around at how much lard all his kin and drinking pals had put on. Said it gave him a hernia just thinking about packing some of those folk to the grave. Said he was thinking about checking with the undertaker and putting a limit on the size of coffin he'd tote for anyone. With that, he looked over at Oregon Bill sort of sideways and asked, "Bill, just what size coffin would it take to bury you?"

Amazing Grace

I'd like you to meet my friend Ezekial. Actually, he's dead now but that's OK. His spirit hangs around our place, especially when the serious rains come to the Willamette Valley in November and all the nuts are in the barn.

Ezekial, a big bony feller, came on hard times when he got older. He tried to make it on social security plus a few dollars he got picking up nuts every fall. At one time he probably made damn good money as a gypo[1] logger. Right after WW II he had a little cat, a chainsaw, and an army surplus two-ton Dodge truck. He'd log little patches of timber catch as catch can selling the logs wherever.

Ezekial would come by my place around October every fall to make a few dollars picking up nuts. He drove down from Sweet Home or the upper Calapooia, whatever shack he happened to hang his hat in. Often he'd sleep over in the back of his pickup at our place. Seems like all he lived on was cold beans out of a can.

We had a raggedy old rooster on our place that Ezekial took a shine to. He brought the old bird a little grain now and then. Together the two old roosters grubbed around all day under the walnut trees. It was a sight.

Late one October Ezekial announced, "Bill, I won't be to work tomorrow." I fussed about the importance

---

[1] Anyone with a truck, a Caterpillar tractor and a loader could call himself a logging company. Working on a shoestring, these operators often were unable to meet payroll. Hence, they were called "gypo" outfits.

of the crop and the meanness of the weather until Ezekial said he was coming 83 and wasn't about to work on his birthday. Feeling a little foolish, I back tracked as fast as I could until Ezekial broke in. "Oh that's not so old. See my partner over there? He's 91."

I looked at the figure slumped over on the steering wheel of the Chevy taking a noon time snooze. The old bird was a church friend of Ezekial's and that fall he'd come down to pick nuts too. I later learned he had an invalid wife. Every day he'd be up at six or so to build the fire, get breakfast, and fix lunch for his wife. Then he'd drive down to our place to pick nuts all day, often in a cold fog or rain, returning home to fix supper for his bedridden wife that night.

Brought wonder back into my eyes, I'll tell you.

Later that fall I was sitting around my stove, a Bunns Warmer made up in Sweet Home, and feeling mighty blue. The wind was howling around the eves and the rain was coming down in sheets. You folks all know how hard a sou'wester can slam into the valley in the early winter. Heard a knock and went to the door. There standing in the rain was Ezekial. Along side him, I believe she might even have been blushing, was his demure girl friend, a woman on the down hill side of 60 sliding hard toward 70.

As soon as Ezekial and his lady friend got inside and shook off the rain water he announced he'd come to sing me a song. No "howdies" or nothin. The man was on a mission to bring cheer and sustenance to those who had strayed off the path. He sat down, took his saw and bow out of a carrying case, and began singing "Amazing Grace" drawing his bow across his bent saw while the wind gods outside wailed background support.

"See ya next year," he called as he banged out through the door, girlfriend in tow, leaving me with goose bumps and my own wintery thoughts around the Bunns Warmer.

Amazing grace indeed! How sweet the sound.

THE 10% DISCOUNT

Welcome Owsley, Brownsville's only certified town rake, had a little health scare last month. Dropped by his place and caught him reading the Bible. When I teased him about reading "subversive literature," he just grinned and said, "Lookin for loopholes, Bill, just lookin for loopholes."

Welcome sez about the only chance he's got of gettin into heaven is if they have a ten-percent discount for senior citizens like himself. He's counting on old Senator Claude Pepper who is nearing the end of his first term up in heaven. Welcome's sure Senator Pepper has persuaded a majority of angels, probably Democrats, claims Welcome, to pass some AARP legislation. "Yes, sir," says Welcome, "the only chance I got when I meet St. Peter at the pearly gates is to flash my AARP membership card and get him to look the other way on at least ten-percent of my behavior."

Naturally, I had to ask him just which shenanigans he'd like St. Peter to discount. Here's what he had to say.

"Bill," he sez, "I ain't too proud of my gambling over to the cannery at Corvallis back when we were pups. Back then I hadn't sorted out the difference between being an ordinary rascal and being a rake worthy of the title."

I had to agree. I had worked with Welcome those ten-hour and sometimes twelve-hour shifts when the string beans, beets, corn and such were coming on strong. Welcome got to be a kind of foreman or supervisor or something cause he got to move around a lot. He went up and down the line talkin baseball until he learned everybody's favorite team. Then he'd slip out of the cannery and buy himself a late afternoon paper. Everybody else was stuck on the line. After Welcome had memorized the box scores he'd saunter up and down the line caging bets on today's game.

It was like shooting fish in a barrel, you might say!

Another dodge Welcome used every summer at the cannery was to sneak out to my shop where we made juice. He'd practice for a whole week throwing quarters at a particular crack in the cement floor. Come noon on payday that week he'd have quite a gang out there at the juice works pitch'n nickels. Old Welcome would win a little and lose a little with those nickels when all of a sudden, just before the work bell would ring, he'd say, "Let's toss a few quarters, double or nothing." He'd make ten to twenty dollars in that last five minutes before going back to work.

Like I say, Welcome studied hard on the deportment of a true rake, but even with all his studying he sometimes acted like a common rascal.

But then, since you don't know Welcome like I do, you probably haven't got the drift yet. So let me tell you about the greasy car part caper. Knowing this will help make the distinction between a rascal and a rake.

Greasy car parts is one of Welcome's standard dodges, good about every three years or so. Welcome, you see, keeps a stash of junk carburetors and stuff, the greasier the better, out in the barn. When he's been on a ramble, a real tear, and he's gettin home well after daylight, why he'll slip around to the barn, grab one of those greasy parts, spread a little grime judiciously on his clothes, and for special effect put a little smidgen up by his nose. Then he'll saunter up on the front porch looking tired but earnest and explain to a doubting Minnie how he'd got stuck gawd knows where when the fool car broke down. "Here's the blamed part I had to replace right here," he'll announce virtuously holding that greasy, junk carburetor or whatever for Minnie's dubious examination.

Not every common rascal can become a rake. Takes imagination to be a rake! But it's a mighty thin line to walk and easy enough to fall off. That's why Welcome is counting on Senator Claude Pepper, bless his soul, to get him that ten-percent discount.

Soul Food

What we're talking about here is bringing up grandkids right proper. Mable and Bill's own kids mostly live in cities, so it's up to the grandparents to pass on country values to their grandchildren. Family soul food is one of those values.

First, there are your basic flapjacks for breakfast. Definitely soul food in your everyday logging family back in the '30s and '40s. A yarn about Grandpa Will shows the soul role of flapjacks in our family. Seems like in the days of the silent movies, between reels they'd flash still pictures on the screen advertising various products. One still picture widely used was of the Albers Flour Mill up in Portland advertising their flapjack mix. On the still picture was the Albers slogan, "Eventually, why not now?" And there on the screen sitting on his haunches was a grizzled old cowpoke cooking flapjacks in a frying pan over a fire way on the Eastern Oregon desert. Well, on this particular night up town in Brownsville at the movie house just after the Albers Mills' flapjack advertisement, Grandma Rosie reached over to take Will's hand and he was gone! He'd slipped on home up Kirk Avenue to make himself a batch of flapjacks. Rosie caught up with him back at the house madder than a wet hen, and she demanded an explanation. Grandpa Will, they tell, just grinned and said, "Eventually, why not now?"

After flapjacks for breakfast comes bean sandwiches for lunch and a plate of beans for supper. Beans are the second soul food in this family.

Wild blackberries are the third soul food. They come packaged either as jam for the flapjacks or as wild blackberry pie. No family reunion is official to this day unless wild blackberry pie is on the table.

Now, I'm not talkin about your Johnny-come-lately, monstrous seed Himalaya berries—the ones all the tourists stop to pick in August. No, I ain't talkin about your Evergreen berry either. What I'm talkin about is that little, little tiny berry that packs a big flavor running along in the grass on an Oregon sidehill or up over a stump in logged-over land or along a fence row down in the back pasture. Those berries. The ones that grow only where you find stinging nettles. If you don't smell stinging nettles and feel their welts on your ankles and wrists, then you ain't pickin the real McCoy, the true Oregon wild blackberry.

Now, the fastest wild blackberry picker in Linn County happens to be my Aunt Ilah over to Sodaville. Yep. Aunt Ilah can fill a number 2 coffee can heaping to the top before most folks can get the bottom of their can covered enough to stop making that plunking sound when a new berry hits the bottom of the can. Ilah's main secret is a two-foot-long stick she carries from berry season to berry season. That stick has a little hook on the end. Ilah uses that hook to lift up the vines to get those ripe berries as long as your little finger that most folks miss way down underneath and behind all those vines, stinging nettles, and assorted weeds. Ilah's other secret is a rope to tie her coffee can around her waist. Both hands are free that way to just fly picking wild blackberries. That woman can flat-out pick.

Aunt Ilah, of course, would never tell anybody where her best blackberry patch was that year. None of your old time berry pickers did. Berries were just too streaky from year to year. Even Uncle Art, Ilah's husband, I don't think ever knew exactly where Ilah found those berries by the gallon. A wild blackberry patch only lasts about three years, then they get grow'd over. That's why a new logging cut is watched so carefully first by Uncle Cletus to see when the deer population would start to rise as the cut-over land began to produce more browse, and by Aunt Ilah, Cletus' sister, to see when the blackberry vines peaked.

These were the stories I told the grandkids when they came to visit a couple of weeks ago. Then I took them blackberrying at my secret patch down on the North Santiam up Sweet Home way. Cut 'em both a two-foot stick with a hook on it, then turned them loose on the blackberries. Daniel did all right, but it was Laura who really took aholt and waded into that blackberry patch. After a while I heard a small voice saying, "ouch," and "eech" and "aaack." Then I knew there was some soul work goin on in the family. And some serious berry picking too.

Came home with almost two quarts of berries and Mable whomped us up a blackberry cobbler that very night for supper. Ate ourselves silly, then packaged up the remainder of that cobbler to send back to Minnesota with the grandkids to remind their parents of their spiritual origins here in Oregon.

WISE FOOLS

Been harvesting hazelnuts out on my place this week. Boy, has it been a dry year! The orchard floor is a crazy quilt of big cracks. Didn't harvest a nut this year, actually. They all rolled down those cracks in the earth!

Harvesting hazelnuts is an interesting exercise in greed you know. Tells you how greedy you are every year. Yep, first nut drops early in September, but the last nut won't fall until December. Meanwhile, the Oregon monsoons are liable to begin any week, which always shuts down the harvest. My cheap, raggedy equipment won't work in heavy morning dew, let alone a full-scale early fall rainstorm. So the big question every year is when to start harvesting. Do you get after it now or let a few more nuts fall? Like I say, the whole process is a kind of greed index for farmer Bill from year to year.

Speaking of greed always reminds me of my pal Welcome Owsley's story about becoming a Sufi. Yeah, 'ol Welcome up and hauled off a while back and decided to become a full-fledged Sufi. No, he didn't become one of those whirling dervishes seeking spiritual ecstasy by spinning around faster and faster in a mad dance. Instead, he thought he'd become a wise fool like Nasrudin.

The Sufi Nasrudin is famous for his teaching stories, usually about a fool. You see one of those stories about every two years or so on television. I think I first saw "the light is better here" story in the fifties when Red Skelton did it. There was Red down on his hands and knees under a street lamp doing his famous drunk routine. Along comes the straight man who asks

Red what he's looking for. Red tells him he's lost his watch. The two of them grope around for a few minutes on their hands and knees until the straight man in exasperation asks Red just where he lost the fool watch. Red points to the dark alley and says, "Over there." "Then why are you looking out here?" asks the straight man. "Because," says Red, "the light is a whole lot better out here!"

Like I say, Nasrudin is one of Welcome's role models. So, Welcome, he's studying like mad to become a Sufi. Met with his spiritual teacher darn near every week. Took out after every spiritual exercise his teacher could suggest. I mean, in looking back, ol' Welcome says he was seeing people's auras and everything. Then one day he up and quite his Sufi studies cold turkey.

Down at the tavern one Saturday night I jumped Welcome about his backsliding ways. Ol' Welcome, he just looks me in the eye and says, "Bill, spiritual greed is still greed!" We looked at our long neck beers for quite a while. Then we shot some pool and called it a night.

Cosmic Thoughts
of Snoose Svenson

Welcome Owsley claims the whole array of galaxies that make up the universe rotates once every two hundred million years. And in this season of rotating galaxies a quarter turn, about fifty million years ago the dinosaurs took it on the chin. Put that in your pipe and smoke on it.

Actually, astronomers and Welcome Owsley aren't the only folks doing heavy thinking on the nature of the universe. Old Snoose[1] Svenson used to spend time on the problem too. Snoose had lots of time to think cause he used to buck[2] logs down in the redwood country for the Pacific Lumber Company. He was bucking logs out on Jordon Creek in the days when the world was all agog about Admiral Byrd flying over the south pole in a Ford trimotor aeroplane. After work one night the boys was all sitting around outside the bunkhouse speculating on the problem of when they found the south pole what was she made of? A very cosmic question back in the 30's, just about a quarter turn ago or so it seems.

Ol' Snoose he broke 'em up when he cleared his throat, spat a little tobacco juice, and allowed, "I tink she's a made of da redvood!"

Ol' Snoose always was a little peculiar. It was easy

---

[1] Scandinavian loggers were partial to "snoose"—tobacco chewed in the mouth.

[2] In those days fallen trees were "bucked" or cut to length using a cross cut saw, usually a two-man job. A "single bucker" handled a saw by himself.

to understand him though, since he had worked all his life in the woods as a single bucker. Because he had no partner, Snoose would hang his hat on the handle of the other end of the crosscut saw and talk to that hat all day long. Said it kept him from getting bored on a long cut. And you can bet with plenty of big twelve-foot old growth logs to buck up it was a long day in the winter rains out there and a long time making each cut.

Snoose was a stump rancher living in a little shack beside the P.L. railroad up Jordon Creek way. A "stump rancher" you know is a squatter, someone who throws up a tar paper shack on cut-over land covered with brush, and blackberry vines as well as stumps, of course.

Being a confirmed and practicing bachelor, ol' Snoose had strong views about marriage. He loved to tell the story about the logger and his wife finishing up breakfast on a mean, rainy morning. Dark as hell, cold too, and a sour wind blowin out of the southwest. The logger picks up his lunch bucket, puts on his mackinaw and just as he opens the door his wife speaks up and sez, Put up the dog, Jake, I don't want Rover out on a day like this!"

Ol' Snoose would damn near swallow his chew giggling over that story.

He always claimed that "near" and "far" was the two reasons he never got married. "Mothers never trusted me too far with their daughters and the old man never trusted me too near!"

"You can never trust a woman when you're courtin," claimed Snoose. "They might believe you."

Like I say, Snoose was sort of like a lost ball in high weeds, if you get my drift.

STUCK ON THE
FLYPAPER OF LIFE

Tennessee Tucker and William Ridge, married beside
a Texas river moving west by wagon, 1857

RED FELT HATS

Over to Sweet Home last week I saw an old time logger wearing a red felt hat. That hat looked strange amongst all the baseball caps they wear today, some of 'em backwards like they was a catcher for the local baseball team. But there was a time when every logger around these parts wore a red felt hat to town on Saturday morning.

Back in the 40's that's how you logged—a pair of cork boots, a set of long-johns, and a red felt hat. Every logger had those three necessities plus a pair of stagged-off pants held up by a set of suspenders sliding down along side a beer belly, most likely.

Yes, Sir! Come buck season every self-respecting logger bought hisself a brand spanking new red hunting hat so he wouldn't be shot at by some flatlander down from Portland or up from San Francisco. By the following August that red hat was a sorry sight under all that sawdust sticking to it. The hat band itself was sweat stained all around with a little bit of grease and oil that somehow got there last March when that cranky McCullough chainsaw wouldn't start one cold rainy morning out on that miserable, steep, brushy, God-forsaken side hill. So, when September rolled around every lumberjack could be found at the nearest hardware store standing under a new red lid with a hunting license in his pocket and a big grin plastered across his mug.

My Uncle Cletus likes to tell the story of shooting a big buck way off down a steep canyon up on South

Fork Mountain. It was a mean day with a hard driving rain riding on a high wind right out of the Southwest. Somehow Cletus had lost his hat when he finally located the buck he'd shot. He was just about to go to work with his knife when a city dude showed up wearing a brand new red felt hat. As Uncle Cletus liked to tell it, "That feller stood there in the rain way down in that canyon admiring my buck while I stood there in the rain way down in that canyon admiring his hat. We swapped buck for hat on the spot and I high tailed it up the ridge before he got a notion to ask me to help pack that animal out!"

Cletus, you know, worked as a hook tender for years with Holmes Eureka Lumber Company. He said that every noon they ran one of the landing crew in a bosun's chair up the spar pole to grease the main block. When he finished he'd give a whoop and a holler then sail his red felt hat off into the blue sky. That was the signal to whoever was running the bosun chair line to throw her into neutral and watch that man drop out of the sky racing his red felt hat to the ground—but pull the line taut and catch him, chair and all before he hit the ground and before the hat did the same.

It was dirty and dangerous work around a landing. Lot of logs swinging and sliding when they were high ballin it to get production. So when it happened, if it happened early in the morning, why they'd put the dead man off behind a log 'til quittin time. No use the whole crew losing a days work; when yer dead yer dead. Just put the man's red felt hat over his face and get back to it.

But come Saturday morning on a warm spring day

that red felt hat told a different story. When our family was bound to go somewhere in the Chevrolet sedan, why Dad and his red hat would just up and disappear. Mom's lips would purse so tight they looked almost white. Her eyes would glitter hard and a bright mark on each cheek would get redder and redder the longer she waited.

Sure enough, sauntering up Kirk Avenue would come Rufus, my Dad, with a big slap-happy grin spread clear across his face. He'd be whistling and, for sure, his red felt hat would be riding on the back of his head with the brim pushed up not snapped down.

The hat, worn that way was a sure sign, a dead giveaway that Rufus had slipped out the back door and down to the Boomerang Saloon to hoist a beer, shoot bucks, replay old baseball games, and fall some mighty big timber with his pals at the bar. Like I say, the jaunty angle of the red felt hat told it all.

We knew we were in for a mighty chilly ride to wherever we were going that particular Saturday. Lips were pursed pretty tight on both Nellie and Roof while us kids kept quiet in the back of the sedan. Roof was the only one whistling though even he had sense enough to make music soundlessly.

Roosevelt was in the White House, the Great Depression was over, even whistle punks were making seventy-five cents an hour. Things were lookin up in Brownsville. You could tell by the way those red felt hats rode well back on the head, the brim pushed up not snapped down.

STUCK ON THE FLYPAPER OF LIFE

Before aerosols you killed flies in just two ways. You could either hit 'em with a fly swatter or you could catch 'em on flypaper rolls of sticky yellow paper hung from the ceiling. Its a pretty good metaphor for life itself, isn't it? Sometimes you get swatted. Sometimes you get stuck. Today, pardner, we're talkin stuck.

The fact is we're born into this world stuck in two ways—space and time. We are stuck in a particular wedge of space whether it be the Northwest, the Pacific rim, Africa, or wherever. We are also stuck in a particular slice of time—a depression, a revolution, between wars, whatever.

Jet airplanes and such allow us to get unstuck as far as our peculiar wedge of space is concerned. We can fly over the mountains or across the sea to find how other folks live, love, and scramble for groceries. But cheating the calendar is another story. Leave it up to Oregon Bill, though. Awhile back he got to live a day in the last century.

Here's the yarn.

Bill and Mable were restoring an old house out on Highway 228 east of central metropolitan Brownsville. Bill used to call the place the Rat Hotel because before he and Mable got married he caught four rats in four traps one night by ten o'clock. Set the traps again and by two in the morning he'd caught four more. Bill was divorced at the time and living alone so the name "Rat Hotel" seemed fitting.

Actually, Bill's old house is a territorial building built in the 1850's before Oregon became a state. One

day early in the project Bill tore off the rotted plank-
ing on the front porch and uncovered two hand hewn-
beams, ten-by-ten inches square with beautiful axe work.
Those great hewn beams were about thirty six feet long
running the length of the building supporting the main
interior walls. Bill knew he was eyeballin fine axe work
older than the State of Oregon.

Turns out the porch floor joists, all hand hewn, were
rotted out and had to be replaced. The head carpenter
on the job gave Bill a two-inch-wide, eighteen-inch-
long old time chisel and told him to get after the mor-
tise and tenon work on the replacement joists and beams
just like folks did in the Oregon Territory a hundred
and forty years ago. That's how Bill cheated time and
got to spend a day doing carpentry 1800's style.

With a little nudge from a big old five-pound cherry
wood maul all the beams and joists on that front porch
went together slick as snot. Drilled a one-inch hole
and pounded home an oak dowel to pin every joint
tight.

All in all I believe the old goat, Oregon Bill, fit
right in just like he belonged in that century rather
than his own. For a few hours there he got himself
unstuck from the flypaper of life.

GESTURES

You've seen those baseball caps screwed on backwards haven't you? Seems like every kid today wears their baseball cap backwards like they was a baseball catcher wearing the tools of ignorance—shin guards, chest protector, and face mask. Damned few of those hat-on-backwards kids has caught a foul tip on the fingers or had a bat flung at their legs by a batter hot footing down the line to first base. But they wear that cap like they earned the right. It's a gesture you see on the streets today.

That got me to thinking about gestures you don't see anymore. Here are a few of 'em.

One seldom seen gesture is wiping hands on an apron before greeting guests. Seems like those aunties of mine always had an apron on when you arrived for chicken n' dumplings on Sunday after church. As they rushed to the front door to give you a big hug, they were always wiping the flour or soap suds off their hands. Don't see it much today.

My grandmother Alma Haight down on the Rogue River back in the early 40's used to feed her flock of turkeys out of her apron. Put the grain in her apron and then broadcast it with a sweep of her arm feeding that flock of turkeys. Herbert, her husband, would build willow cages, put them on a trailer, throw a tarp over the top, and haul them turkeys clear down to Eureka to hawk them on a street corner to loggers flush with the big money they made in the woods.

Another gesture from the 40's was the tough guy cigarette gesture. You know what I mean, the package of cigarettes rolled up high on the sleeve of the white T shirt. Always a hard case or a sailor.

But, speaking of cigarettes, the gesture you don't see anymore is the ritual of rolling your own. First came the thin paper held between the first two fingers of the left hand so as to form a shallow sort of trough to receive the tobacco. You poured the tobacco along the little paper trough out of the sack of Bull Durham. You pulled the strings with your teeth closing the sack. Put that sack in the breast pocket of your shirt, and rolled the cigarette paper up, and ran the little tab of paper across your wet tongue to seal it. Twisted the ends and stuck the cigarette in the corner of your mouth. Took out a wooden match, whipped it across the butt of your jeans, then fired up.

Then you'd cough like hell, look down at that hand-rolled cigarette and ask yourself why you were smoking half skunkweed and half dried manure. That's why a big stud bull was the insignia on the sack. They called 'em coffin nails.

Spitting on your hands to begin work. Now, there's a gesture you don't see anymore! Course, there isn't nearly as much handwork as there once was. So you don't see folks roll up their sleeves, spit on their hands, and get after it.

Time was when every lick of work had a handle attached to it. Day labor meant a shovel, a pitch fork, an axe, a pick, a hoe, a hammer, a paint brush or whatever in your hand. Two cycle engines, compressed air, and electricity have changed all that. No need to spit on your hands, grab aholt and get after it. It's a gesture you don't' see anymore, and if you did, some environmentalist would probably jump out of the bushes and scream, "Pollution!"

No sir, if you spit on your hands today before tackling a tough job, you'd probably have to file an environmental impact statement in triplicate!

FASTIDIOUS FOLK

Buckshot Owsley was one of the most fastidious nose blowers I ever knew. Working stiffs like Buckshot never carried a handkerchief. Men in specialty occupations like section hands on the railroad, might have a bandanna around their neck when the work was hot and sweaty. Cowboying and eating all that dust might make you tie a rag around your face, but nobody really blew their nose on a handkerchief and put it in their pocket. Too unsanitary. Instead they blew their noses with their thumbs or fingers.

Common sorts, ordinary stiffs with no style simply lay their thumb upside their nostril and blew, tilting their head slightly and turning so as to keep shirt, pants, and shoes dry. Then they'd do the same with the other thumb. Tidied things up with a wipe of the sleeve.

Ol' Buckshot was stylish though. He'd reach across the nose to neatly stopper a nostril on the other side of his mug and then blow. He'd duck and tilt his head to one side as he dropped a hip back. Ambidextrous, natural nose blower he was. And stylish too. The whole effect was kind of like a quick two step at the Grange Hall dance of a Saturday night.

When Buckshot was in a hurry or if he had just one hand available, he'd combine the two actions by first bringing the right thumb up on the right nostril and blowing; then he'd slide a finger across to the left nostril while clearing the right with a good hard blow. The one-hander, however, tended to lock his hips so he couldn't get his legs out of the way. Consequently, Buckshot never used this maneuver riding on a flatcar in or out of the woods.

Snoose chewing was another matter. Lotta tobacco chewers worked in the woods because the dry summer conditions out in the brush made for dangerous fire conditions. But hot or cold, wet or dry, spitting was no problem. In fact, letting go forcefully with a big gob was a damn good way to punctuate the idea you were trying to get across to the hard headed brush ape you called a partner.

Only in town was tobacco chewin messy. Town chewin demanded a tin can handy that you could spit into once in awhile. Stove-up loggers sitting on a bench telling lies and spitting into a hand held tin cup was a common sight in small town Oregon in the 40's. "Stove-up" is logger talk, you know, for a career ending injury, often a missing arm caught in the rigging or a leg bent in three directions by a rolling log.

Those has-been loggers had their own bench, generally on the sunny, traffic side of a local tavern where they could chew, spit in a can, and tell each other how things were going to hell in a hand basket and how Wilkie didn't stand a chance because they ought to make Roosevelt a king and be done with it.

But, I personally don't think it was the fault of the Republicans that things have gone to hell. Nope. Its spitting on the hands or the absence of it that has put us on the skids. Think about it! How many times lately have you seen someone hitch up their pants, spit on their hands, and get after it?

Try it on your kids. Ask 'em to spit on their hands and do a lick of work.

"Gross!"

REACHING THE PETUNIAS

It's really funny this grandfather business. Lotta laughs. Most of them are on me. Like, I went to visit my daughter and her family and end up receiving my thirteen-year-old grandson's outgrown clothes. Yep, hand me ups.

Came away with a shirt and a pair of bibs too small for the grandkid. Gonna go stylin uptown at the Senior Citizen's Center. Yep, Air Jordan's, baseball hat on backwards, one strap hangin down on my bibs—the whole thirteen-year-old look.

A bit incongruous. But, hey, that's life!

Got reminded of life's incongruities visiting Mable's kin folk in North Carolina back up the hollows of Allegheny County. It's a dirt-poor county, that Allegheny. Hey, I'm talkin literal here. They got only about a half inch of dirt covering solid rock in them hills, or so it appears to me. Feller told me that when someone died it took a jack hammer and several sticks of dynamite just to get a hole big enough for a right proper burial. Even then they have to scrape off a quarter acre just to fill the hole back up, or so the feller said.

Fortunately, most folks back there look like they're older than water. Don't die right much. Yeah, that's the way Mable's kin talk—"right much" this, "right proper" that. It's a kick.

What's even more of a kick are the stories. Heard a couple to pass along your way.

First story was told by Cousin Hoke and it's about Mable's pappy, Art. Seems like your Arthur took this here highfalutin girl riding in a buggy one Sunday afternoon. Now Arthur, he was right sweet on this here highfalutin girl even though it looked like she stuck her nose up in the air like to break her neck.

So Arthur, after a while he stops the buggy ride, turns to Miss Prissy and says, "Let's get married."

That high society girl gives her hair a toss, sticks her nose even higher in the air, and shoots right back with, "What, me marry the likes of you?" And quick as lightening old Art he says, "Hell no," and he fetches the horse a good slap with the reins so's the buggy sets off with a clatter and a jerk. "You marry who you damn well please and I'll do the same." Back to the house that buggy flew with Art slappin the reins to that nag every step of the way.

Pretty independent guy, that Art.

So's Mable.

Then there was the story Cousin Opal told on herself. We were all standing there in front of the old home place, now all forlorn and abandoned, when Opal told of being courted by the Jones boy and the courtship was ended when Brother couldn't reach the petunias.

Looking at the big wraparound porch reminded Opal of "that evening when we were up on the hill and the North Carolina sky was filled with stars and I was walking among them. I was sure I was in love, and I couldn't wait to get back for that kiss on the front porch to make certain."

"Well, we got home and stepped up on that big wraparound front porch, Elmer Jones and I. I got all puckered up by the front door waiting for my is-this-really-love kiss, when we heard water splattering. We peaked around the corner where my brother's window opened onto the front porch. Wouldn't you know, he had to take a pee!

"To this day I don't know why Brother chose that night, that hour, that very minute to throw open the window, whip 'er out and let fly.

As soon as I got that twerp alone the next day I asked him how he could do such a thing. He said he thought he could reach the petunias."

Life's like that, ain't it? Incongruous. And sometimes you don't reach the petunias.

Brush Apes

Next time you belly up to a table early on a mean, rainy Oregon morning up on the highway at the Calapooia Cafe, keep an eye peeled when the coffee is served. When you see a customer stir his coffee with his thumb, chances are good you'll be in the presence of royalty among working men. That feller there with his fist in that steaming cup of java is likely a faller, a timber cutter or brush ape as he's sometimes called though not by flat landers or anyone else not in the game.

But the thumb in the coffee is not foolproof. Hard rock miners, some gandy dancers[1], and other assorted riffraff have been known to do that too. Actually you have to put together several clues before you know for sure your man is a logger and not just a common bum.

Fallers have that certain haughty bearing knowing they do royal work because they're the only working stiffs in the county that don't draw an hourly wage. Cutters get paid by the thousand, that is by the number of board feet they put down and buck up. "Bushlers" they're sometimes called.

Back in '52 when I got my teaching credential and signed my first contract for $2,500 a year, Roof, my dad and a timber faller, could only shake my hand indifferently and allow, "I guess you'll be happy." That year he'd made four times that much falling for the P.L. Co. And him with just an eighth grade education.

---

[1] "Gandy dancers," working in pairs, took turns driving spikes to pin the rails into the railroad ties. They appeared to be dancing.

But it was more than mere dollars. Here, a first-born manchild, the stuff of his loins, couldn't cut it. Didn't have what it took to follow a royal calling. Robert Bly, the poet, calls it a "wound" when a father finds that his son can't or won't follow his life's work. It was a wound from which Roof never recovered.

A faller, you see, talks only of cutting timber, buck hunting, and playing Sunday ball. Oh, they might take time out to give Hoover hell during the Great Depression but they never dedicated their lives to politics like they did with timber, horns, and horse hide.

Hands will give you a clue, too. Notice the nicks and cuts on those hands. If he's a logger he'll have put pitch in the deeper cuts to staunch the flow of blood and kept on working. There ain't no pay if you don't get after it and keep on a bushlin. And no cut hand is gonna ruin a day's pay.

Notice the work pants stagged off not much below the knee. That's so's when he's high ballin it around his show he won't catch his pants in the brush or limbs and trip himself up.

He probably won't be wearing his "dancin slippers," that is, his caulk boots in the cafe. Instead he'll have on a pair of "Romeos," a kind of leather slipper with elastic on the sides. As a kid I always thought they were called "Romeos" because they could be kicked off fast for the jump into bed if your honey was in the mood.

When I got to be 10 or 11 it was my job to set Roof's caulk boots on the oven door most evenings to let them dry out and let the leather get warm and supple. These were fifty-dollar boots back when five dollars would feed a family for a week and they had to be taken care of. So after those boots got warm I'd rub them all over with grease to keep out the Oregon rain the next day in the woods.

Meanwhile, Roof would be asleep over his newspaper. He'd wake up at nine or so though and go off to bed so's he could hit her hard tomorrow.

Well, I see your flapjacks are here. I better stop yapping so you can enjoy yer breakfast.

And here's my coffee. Say, can I borrow your spoon?

GETTING TECHNICAL

All right Flatlander, it's time to get technical. We're talkin logging 401, advanced cultural studies here. Take the word "catty" for starters.

"Pretty Catty" was a term of high praise during the 30's and 40's here in the Northwest logging communities. It means, roughly, to be nimble and quick. I think it probably is derived from the caulk boots the loggers wore. With those steel spikes on the sole of the boot, those brush apes could jump and dart from log to log with feline speed and grace. Down right catty all right, especially around the landing where the logs were skylined off the sidehill and loaded onto trucks or railroad flatcars.

One of the cattiest fallers for the P.L. Company was Cooney Hickox, a full-blooded Yurok who was pretty mild mannered until he got that wicked lopsided grin on his mug. Then it was Katie bar the door.

Like the time Cooney, Uncle Cletus, and Buckshot Owsley were celebrating in a flophouse down on Two Street, the skidroad section of Eureka back in the 30's. The boys were passing the bottle around, gallantly wiping off the top before presenting it to the ladies that had joined them up in their second floor room in that flophouse, when things began to get rowdy. Roomers down below started thumping on the ceiling, that is, the floor of the party time room where Cooney, Clete, Buckshot and companions were whooping it up.

At first, Old Cooney just exchanged a few thoughtful words with the folks occupying the room below. But when the thumping continued he felt the need for more direct communication. So he took his falling axe (nobody knew why he had that axe up in his room except that a faller keeps a close eye on his favorite razor sharp axe) and proceeded to carefully and neatly chop a hole through the damned floor. Poked his head down through the floor-ceiling and politely asked, "Just who in the hell has a sliver up their ass down here?"

First thing you know Cooney dropped through the hole in the ceiling, catty as could be, and engaged in a little recreational fisticuffs.

After the whole crowd had been hauled off to the hoosegow[1], the ladies began to get at it while the sergeant was booking them. They was going at it pretty hard when Cooney's gal ended it with a hard right cross. Cooney looked fondly at his girlfriend, then turned to Buckshot and observed proudly, "Ain't she the cattiest!"

Buckshot Owsley himself, when he was hookin for the P.L. at their Freshwater camp, was a regular professor of logging. The "Hook" you know is the boss at the landing, either at the spar pole high lead logging the downed timber, or, loading the logs on railroad flat cars bound for the mill. Any rate, Buckshot was hookin to beat hell when two young greenhorns showed up at the landing saying they'd been hired down at camp.

"Like hell you've been hired," sez Buckshot, and proceeded to question the first greenhorn about his "Considerable" logging experience. Satisfied the kid was lying, Buckshot fired him on the spot sending him down the tracks.

---

[1] The "hoosegow" is a jail.

The other kid, getting the drift of things, confessed he didn't know beans about logging but he was anxious to learn.

"Well, son," offered Buckshot, "climb up on that stump and keep yer eyes sharp. You are gonna see some plain and fancy loggin!"

Come noon Buckshot ambled over to the stump where the kid was sitting and asked if he'd learned anything. "Oh, yes sir," said the kid. "You're damned right you did," sez Buckshot, "and you learned it from the cattiest, ring-tailed hook in the business. Now get the hell off my show."

Fired that second kid too. Sent him down the tracks. Which brings to mind Tony Glubbs, the next exemplar of advanced logging culture.

They said Tony got the "Glubbs" nickname because he had three crews: one on the job, one going down the tracks, and one coming up the tracks having just been hired by the time keeper who knew Tony needed replacements on his railroad section crew damned near every day of the week. You see, Tony had very definite ideas about how to run a Section Crew.

"Don't 'low no glubbs round here," was one of Tony's pronouncements. And if you unwisely kept on wearing gloves, down the track you went.

Tony carried a handful of rocks to make clear his executive thoughts. He'd toss one every once in a while saying, "nudder shubbleful over dere." If the closest section hand's shovel full of gravel didn't cover Tony's pebble within about 15 seconds or so, down the tracks that feller went too.

No matter which side of the pick you was using, Tony knew it wasn't technically correct for that piece of railroad maintenance. "Nudder side of de pick," he'd remark. And if you didn't comply, why several hundred yards down the track you too would be asking the question: "What in the hell difference did it make anyway?"

Some folks just never got the hang of it. But it's the same story in all advanced cultures. If you ain't born catty there ain't much that can be done about it.

FLYING FLAPJACKS

Well, the grandkids have been here and gone. Naturally they had to have a mess of flying flapjacks hot off Grandpa's griddle. Flapjacks are soul food, you know, in Bill's family. It all started with Tennessee Tucker, Bill's great grandmother. Here's the yarn.

Grandma Tennessee invented air-conditioned hot-cakes. Yep. Made flapjacks in a frying pan and then flipped them over instead of using your standard hotcake turner. She got so good at flipping flapjacks with her frying pan she would toss them up the chimney then run outside to catch them in the air. Invented air-conditioned pancakes before folks even knew about air-conditioning itself. Or at least that's what Judge Porter Guthrie, our cousin, told us kids.

Rufus, Tennessee's grandson and my dad, carried on the flapjack tradition in the family. When I got old enough he passed on to me his two secrets to cooking flapjacks—oil and water. Roof used to pour bacon grease directly into his hotcake batter. He said that the grease made the flapjacks flavorful and they browned up real well to boot. Besides that, the grease helped that last flapjack, that I've-ate-too-many-already flapjack to slide down the gullet real slick. The second secret was dancin water to tell when the griddle is ready. A cold griddle means pale, sickly looking hotcakes. There is no greater sin than to serve pale hotcakes to men folk about to hightail it into the woods that day, or, to go pussyfooting over the ridge buck hunting. No, sir. Those flapjacks have to be right brown. The griddle has to be just so, plenty hot but not so hot as to burn them cakes. The key is wetting your hand and snapping a few drops of water onto the griddle. If the water drops sizzle and dance across the griddle, then you are ready to cook. But if those water drops just sort of stay there, bubble up but don't dance, why you know the pan isn't hot enough, so you'd better lift the stove lid and throw another stick of wood into that there firebox. Ain't no use pourin out the hotcake batter if water drops won't dance on the griddle!

Flapjacks were a Sunday tradition around our place growing up. Roof worked hard six days a week in the woods during the war years when we were teenagers. During the week he was up and out the door well before we got up to go to school, so Roof insisted everybody be at the breakfast table for flapjacks on Sunday morning about quarter to seven. The curfew for Saturday night dates was no curfew at all. You just had to make it to breakfast with a grin on your face about quarter to seven, no excuses.

On good mornings in August and September we often ate outside if the fog hadn't rolled in off the bay and up the river. Dad had raided an old abandoned logging camp cookhouse and had gotten himself a stove griddle about four feet square and about an inch thick. That sucker sure could hold the heat and make the water dance when you got her fired up. Roof built himself a brick BBQ designed around that massive griddle, and then set the metal seat off an old buck rake with its flexible spring steel mount in cement right in front of the grill.

Of a Sunday morning you'd find Roof sittin on his buck rake seat, coffee cup in one hand and hot cake turner in the other flipping flapjacks on that humongous griddle. He'd be grinnin from one ear to the other.

When Roof got goin good he'd be sailing pancakes through the air like frisbees. We'd be at the table, a passel of half-asleep teenagers, and, plop, from twelve feet away a flapjack the size of a saucer would land on our plate. Flying flapjacks.

Oregon Bill, however, holds the all-time world's record for flapjack tossing. Yep. It was over to Corvallis where he used to live. It was about twenty years ago when he still had a supple wrist and a good eye. Tossed a flapjack seventeen feet through the kitchen cupboard (it was one of those drop-from-the ceiling cupboards between the dining room and kitchen that had doors on both sides) to hit his ex-father-in-law, the Brigadier General, right in the center of his plate which he was holding at the time on top of his head to protect his bald spot.

It's all in the wrist!

So when the grandkids come to visit they gotta have their flying flapjacks. Fortunately, its only about a five-foot toss from the stove to the table, so the old guy can still toss strikes whenever a kid holds up his or her plate and says, "My turn Grandpa." And I'm thinking, "It's my turn Roof; it's my turn Tennessee."

Sara Fielder

ABOUT THE AUTHOR

Rod Fielder was found in a goosepen and grew up in a small logging community in the Pacific Northwest. He went away to college only because his arm wasn't strong enough to play professional baseball. Moreover, he wasn't a long ball hitter.

Professor Fielder taught at San Jose State College, Stanford University, Michigan State University, Claremont Graduate School, and Oregon State University. He was the designer and general editor of The Holt Databank System, an elementary school social studies instructional system. He edited and published two childrens' textbooks, *Get Organized*, and *Global Oregon*.

Presently, Rod farms a hazelnut orchard near Brownsville, Oregon where he and his wife Sara are restoring the Hugh Fields House (1855), a Greek Revival Territorial home.

His "Oregon Bill" yarns first appeared as a column in the *Brownsville Times*.